NO IRE

BY **CARVER CANE**

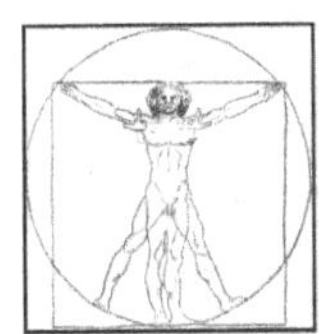

STONE Pulp Press
STONEPULP.COM

Stone Pulp Press
Hanover, MA
WWW.STONEPULP.COM

This is a work of fiction, any resemblance to actual people or events is coincidental.

LCCN: 2024939771
ISBN: 979-8-9898749-2-7

Dedicated to the Polish serial killer
who brought this story to my attention.

Disclaimer: Everything in this story is true (except for this statement). Due to the newsworthy nature of what is depicted, most names have remained unchanged. All facts have been verified via alternative news outlets and an extensive porn collection.

Chapter 1

____

The following events began on June 24th, 2022.

She was a woman in her forties, but could take any man from zero to a hundred in no time at all. He was Vincenzo Longhorn, the man whose epic member—featured on covers of VHS tapes found under counters and in secret rooms of 1990s video stores—could stop a girl cold. They sat in the partial shadows of a back booth. The one furthest from the bar and the front entrance. The kind of booth with the wrap-around seat. A place to hide and scheme. A place to hate. And a place to love. They were doing it all.

"It's so big," She said.

"Twelve lethal inches of power," he said.

"I thought it was bigger."

"That's pretty freaking big."

"It's so hard."

"Wouldn't really work if it wasn't," he said.

"Is it ready and loaded?"

"Always is. Just waiting for you to tell me what you want me to do with it."

"You know what I want," she said. Leaning closer to him, closer to it. She glanced away and then said, "Here comes the waitress, get it off the table."

With surprising quickness, Vincenzo slid the impressive weapon off the table, returning it between his legs.

The waitress stopped beside their table and eyed them suspiciously. They didn't know she eyed everyone suspiciously; after all, only suspicious people came into that bar. And as for the back booth, the only people who sat there were guilty as hell. She grimaced, seeing the man's hands below the table, remembering that the Mexican kid who usually mopped up the blood and semen left behind each night had disappeared. Now it was up to her to do it, and she contemplated asking Big Hal for the extra two dollars an hour he'd paid the kid. But not being sure if it was ICE that made the kid disappear, she kept her mouth shut.

"Another round of drinks?" the waitress asked.

"Yes, please," the woman sitting at the table said. Her eyes glinted like light off hot, polished steel, and her pressed smile hid secrets only the devil could deduce. "Another martini," she said.

The waitress eyed the man, not realizing she was eyeing porn royalty. Not realizing what was held below that table. "You?" the waitress said to him.

"Yeah," he said.

"Another water?" the waitress said, as if questioning his manhood. If she only knew.

"Soda water," the man corrected. "With a twist," he added.

The waitress smirked and walked away, her hips wagging like a scolding finger.

The woman at the table turned back to Vincenzo, her eyes like animals looking to devour him. "Can I see it again?"

"She'll be back soon," he said, nodding toward the waitress.

The woman reached under the table and began caressing the hard steel. "Tell me what you're going to do with this again," the woman said, her voice laced with desire.

"Tell me what you want me to do with it," he said.

"You *know* what I want," she said, leaning forward, brushing her lips against his.

"I'm not sure I do," he said.

"Then maybe I heard wrong about the great Vincenzo Longhorn."

"Depends what you heard."

"I heard he knew how to use this thing. But maybe you're no longhorn after all."

"The longhorn is accurate."

"Maybe what you thought was a longhorn was nothing but an udder." The weapon twitched under the table. She gripped it tighter. "Maybe instead of Vincenzo Longhorn, you should be called Bessie the Milking Cow?"

"Stop it."

"Bessie the Milking Cow starring in *Udder Desire*?"

"Do you want me to get mad?" he said.

"Maybe," she said.

"Then, *enough*," he hissed.

The waitress returned and set their drinks on the table. When the man and woman at the table didn't acknowledge her, the waitress walked away, her wagging hips now a middle finger.

Vincenzo and the woman stared at one another. His expression heated almost to a rolling boil. Her expression smooth as ice.

She let go of the weapon between his legs and said, "Let me see it again."

"You don't deserve to," he said.

"Deserving is subjective," she said.

"I thought deserving is the reason we're here."

"There are those who deserve satisfaction," she said.

"And those who deserve denial," he said.

"Do I really deserve more denial?"

"I think maybe you're confusing deserve with desire."

"Are you going to deny me my desire for satisfaction?"

"Do you deserve that satisfaction?"

"Do I deserve my desire for satisfaction?"

"Hold on, do you deserve the denial of satisfaction, or do you deserve the satisfaction of what someone else deserves?"

"I'm not sure I follow. Who is the someone else who deserves something?"

"I thought we were talking about your husband?"

"My husband? How did he get into this?"

"I thought we were talking about you deserving your desire of the satisfaction of getting what your husband deserves?"

"*I* get what my husband deserves?"

"No, he gets what *he* deserves."

"I deserve for my husband to get what he deserves?"

"Yes."

"Then, yes."

"Wait, you're saying yes to…?" He stopped, looked at the ceiling, and then said, "Look, do you want me to kill your husband or not?"

"Yes," she said, caressing the weapon beneath the table. "Now can I see it?"

He shifted, pulling the weapon from between his legs.

"What is it called again?" she said.

"It's a .44 Magnum, baby, like the one Dirty Harry used."

With a flash of gunmetal, the weapon was almost on the table again when she stayed his hand. "Here comes the waitress again."

As he returned the weapon under the table, a loud clap of thunder filled the bar.

Vincenzo and the woman looked at one another as a wisp of white smoke wafted from beneath the table, and Vincenzo said, "I think I might've just shot my dick off."

"Seriously? Your dick again?"

Chapter 2

One Week Prior

The blonde with blue eyes sat, prim, proper, quiet—the good girl, legs crossed, hands folded in her lap. The stage was empty. For now. But soon he would be up there, the answer to her desires.

The blue-eyed woman shifted on the folding metal chair, partly to be sure she could see the stage better, partly to get the blood flowing again in her perfectly shaped butt cheek. Her ass, which, when used right, literally stopped traffic—foot and automobile traffic alike.

Fellow attendees shuffled to the other metal chairs. A woman plopped down in the seat in front of her, causing the blonde with blue eyes to have to shift in the other direction. This woman reeked of cigarette smoke and had hair the color and consistency of a scarecrow's. Her attitude pronounced a belief that her own ass stopped traffic, but hers was the kind that got it moving again. This woman turned and said, "I'm so excited."

"Me, too," the blue-eyed woman said.

"I'm a huge fan of his."

"As am I."

"Really?" The scarecrow woman eyed her, ogling her perfect hair, the long legs emerging from her straight, hip-hugging skirt, and the conservative, pressed blouse with one button too many open at the neckline.

"Oh, yes. He has talents beyond compare."

"I'll say," the scarecrow woman said. "And he can act. Like really act, right?"

"Absolutely," the blue-eyed woman said. She glanced up at the empty stage again, being sure there was a clear line of vision.

The scarecrow woman said, "Like in that movie he did with Gina Parks and Trudi Welles, where she played the gumshoe and he played the hellion cop."

"*Dick Me, My Darling?*"

"Yeah, that's it. That was like a real film no ire."

"No ire?"

"Yeah, it's a type of movie. Usually like detectives and such."

"You mean noir?"

"No, I mean no ire. It's spelt n-o-i-r-e."

"I don't think it has an e, and I'm pretty sure it's pro-nounced noir." She glanced at the empty stage again.

"Well there certainly ain't no w in it, missy." The scarecrow woman stared at her like a nun spotting someone mouthing the wrong prayer in church.

"Okay," the blue-eyed woman said, quietly gathering her bag and craning her neck to spot another seat. She needed the perfect angle to fully see the stage.

The scarecrow woman, still staring, said, "Noewar? That don't make no sense. So don't get all high and mighty on me."

"Excuse me, I think I see a better seat." She stood and headed to another row.

The woman called from behind her, "You know what does have a w? Whore. You whore."

As the blue-eyed woman shuffled down the aisle of chairs, she saw him. He stood in the corner of the hall talking to two old women. These old women looked more like leaders of a knitting circle than custodians of a sexual discovery seminar.

The blue-eyed woman stopped and stood still in the middle of the aisle. His eyes met her eyes. A crackle of energy went through the air.

One of the old women turned on the microphone and blew into it, tapping its head gently. "Okay, now," the woman said. "Testing?" She caressed the tip of the microphone again. "We should all be finding our seats now. Testing?"

Their eyes never lost contact as she continued to an empty seat and sat, causing him to crane his neck to keep eye contact. A puppy searching for its master.

"All right, ladies…testing?" the woman said. She blew the microphone again. "Is this working?" she whispered to him.

"I believe so," he said, still staring into desire, the blue diamond eyes staring back at him.

"All right, ladies. Ladies?" the old woman with the microphone said, talking over the murmur of lingering conversation. "Ladies?"

The murmur ended.

"Thank you for coming, ladies…and gentlemen? I don't see any gentlemen. Okay. Welcome to the Saint Vincent Tabernacle's continuing series on self-discovery. Oh my, this is a much bigger crowd than our Praying and Mindfulness seminar we had last week." She giggled and said, "Are you ready to have some fun?"

The ladies in the seats cheered and whooped.

"Oh my," the old woman chuckled. "That was quite a response. Today's event will be…" she squinted through her oversized glasses as she now read from an unfolded piece of paper, "…an afternoon of sexual discovery. Oh, deary," she said, turning over the paper to see if something else was written on the back. When she saw it was blank, she continued reading the front, "So please welcome the…beast that won't cease? The python you all want to choke on? The hulking hero who will keep you…cumin? cue-ming…?" the old woman said, turning toward the man and pointing to the mispronounced word.

"That's cumming," he said.

"Oh, okay. He will keep you coming—with a u apparently—back for more." Her granny voice faltered as she squinted harder at the page. "He is the star of such classic films as…" she squinted more, her voice reading more slowly. "*Pool Table Orgy*? Oh dear. *Anal Blaster Part 3*? *Bondage Butts and Bukake*? Did I pronounce that right?" she whispered to him.

He nodded.

She continued reading, "*Dick Me, My Darling*—that one doesn't sound so bad—and…oh…and, *Hot Wet Fuck Sluts Taking it up the Ass While Sucking Monster Cocks and Licking Luscious Creamy Cum-Filled Squirting Pussies*. Oh, my, that was a mouthful," the old woman said.

"You should see the movie," he said.

"Oh, okay," she said to him, then she announced, "Ladies and gentle…ladies, please…" She cleared her throat and said, "Ladies, please…rock that cock and welcome Vincenzo Longhorn."

The women cheered and began chanting: "Rock that cock. Rock that cock. Rock that cock…."

Vincenzo Longhorn snatched the microphone from the old woman and ran up onto the stage. Cheers and whooping broke through the rock-that-cock chanting. Vincenzo smiled and patted his hand in the air to quiet the crowd.

"Okay, okay, ladies. Grazie. Grazie," he said, his accent as Italian as Andy Garcia. "Thank you for all that, you lovely ladies, all. I am here to help you. Help you all find that desire you crave."

His eyes fell onto the blue gems of her eyes again, and he paused. He was the deer in her headlight eyes.

Another woman, the one with the scarecrow hair, broke him from his trance when she called, "Show us your dick."

Several women whooped like birds calling for their dinner.

Vincenzo laughed and smiled, saying, "No, no, now, ladies, we aren't here for that."

"Yeah we are," the woman with the scarecrow hair called back.

"No, no, we are here to talk about—"

Several boos spattered the crowd.

"Show us your dick," the woman with the scarecrow hair said again.

"We want the beast," another shouted.

"Ladies, please—"

The chant of "Rock that cock," broke out again.

"Ladies, I—"

"Rock that cock. Rock that cock. Rock that cock…"

His eyes fell on her eyes again.

She arched an eyebrow.

"Okay, okay," he said. He reached toward his pants' zipper. The women whooped and cheered. He stayed his hand, his fingers outstretched before the zipper like a promise. "But not yet," he said.

"Awwww," the crowd bellowed as one voice.

"We are here to explore sexual discovery," he said. He began striding across the stage like a caged tiger, and gesturing his hands to emphasize each word. "And that exploration of sexual discovery can lead to the courage of all kinds of *self*-discoveries. Think about it, what holds us back from exploring what we really want in life? Societal taboos? Fear of judgment? Religious oppression?" He gestured around the tabernacle and glanced toward the old women now standing in the back corner.

The old women smiled and waved back.

"Family *values*?" he said, and on the word *values* he made air quotes. "But what about *your* values? What about *your* wants? What about *your needs*? Not just surface needs, like I need to get to work. I need to make dinner. I need to mow the lawn and feed the dog. I mean real inner, deep, to-the-core *needs*. What about the things that raise your pulse and send butterflies scattering though your entire body?"

The crowd of women nodded. Some humming agreement.

Vincenzo continued to stride across the stage, gripping the microphone tight, and said, "Well ask for it, ladies. Don't be afraid. Ask for it. Get it. Take it."

"Yeah," some of the women said.

"They're *your* needs. No one else is going to do it. *You* need to get them."

"Yeah," the women said.

"Let me tell you a story about a girl. Some of you might know her. Her name was Havana."

A few women whooped.

"At one time, she was the biggest star in adult movies. But that wasn't always the case. She was timid at first. Hesitant. But then she started to branch out, and we as an audience began to witness her own sexual discovery on film. We were able to see her awakening. We watched her blossom. In fact, I did one of her first anal scenes with her."

A few whoops from the crowd.

"Think about that?" he said, cupping his massive member. "Talk about diving into the fire, am I right?"

A few more women whooped. A few offered empathic grimaces.

He stopped his striding and said, in a slightly softer voice, "She shot herself not long after that. Which kind of always bothered me…I mean, it wasn't because of that scene…I don't think it was, anyway…. She was a really nice person. Like legitimately the sweetest person in the world…." He stared off to the back of the room. "I mean, I guess it wasn't really self-discovery if she was told to do it. I remember how nervous she was, and…they kind of exploited her, using her sweetness like that…." He paused, as if somehow focusing beyond the back wall. "And I guess, technically, I'm exploiting her now even bringing this up…" He glanced around the room at the staring faces. "We're *all* still exploiting her, aren't we…?"

The room was silent as a confessor awaiting penance. The women looked at one another, looked at some of the religious artifacts scattered about the room. Some bent their heads in self-reflection.

"Show us your dick," the woman with the scarecrow hair shouted.

"Rock that cock. Rock that cock. Rock that cock…" The rest of the women joined in. "Rock that cock. Rock that cock. Rock that cock…"

He glanced at the woman with the blue eyes again, and her arched eyebrow. She shrugged, daring him.

In one smooth motion, like a matador flourishing his cape, he unzipped and let loose the dangling coils of his beast.

The crowd erupted, on their feet cheering. He glanced at the blue eyes and arched eyebrow, and he saw a wry smile spread across her lips. He then saw, over her shoulder, the old woman staring at his exposed monster cock. Her eyes rolled back and she fainted away into a heap.

"Shit," he said.

Chapter 3

The blue-eyed woman stood in front of the tabernacle, mulling around the main entrance, extracting a cigarette from a platinum case. She brought the cigarette to her lips, but before she could flick her lighter, a flame erupted before her eyes. She saw a gold zippo, and his large hands with their long, thick fingers holding it.

"Looks like we're the last two in the world," Vincenzo said, lighting her cigarette.

She took a drag and blew it out the side of her mouth. With her two fingers delicately holding her cigarette, she gestured to the rest of the gathering crowd and said, "Seems we aren't alone."

"I meant the last two smokers," he said, lighting his own cigarette.

"Something tells me that woman might be a smoker," she said, nodding toward the woman with the scarecrow hair.

The woman with the scarecrow hair stared back at her, the scarecrow's brow falling over her eyes in an avalanche of hatred, her mouth pouted like a child about to end the game and take her ball home.

"Do you know her?" he said.

"We talked briefly before you took the stage. Not a fan."

"You're not a fan of her, or she's not a fan of you?"

She flicked her eyes to meet his and blew out another stream of smoke. "A little of both, I suppose."

"The look she's giving you, I'd say she's less of a fan of you."

"It's all right. After all, looks don't kill."

"Are you sure about that?"

She blew out another stream of smoke. "So I've heard."

"Do you have a lot of fans?" he said.

"A few."

"Would you like one more?"

They turned to face one another now, each taking a step closer to sense their radiating body heat.

"Maybe," she said.

"Maybe," he said.

"Maybe I don't have as many fans as you do." She gestured at the women mulling around the front of the tabernacle.

He shrugged and said, "Well I—" He was cut off when a paramedic squeezed between them.

"Okay, folks, step aside, please."

Two more paramedics wheeled the old woman out on a gurney. The old woman moaning, and saying, "It was huge. It was unnaturally huge. That was not of this world. It—that's him," she said, as the gurney wheeled between Vincenzo and the blue-eyed woman. "That's him."

As the old woman passed between them, Vincenzo and the blue-eyed woman let loose a stream of smoke, which engulfed the old woman.

"He has Satan's co—" the old woman squealed, but her statement was lost in smoke as a coughing fit took hold of her.

The paramedics wheeled her off toward the waiting ambulance.

"You remind me of a young Janine Lindemulder," he said.

"I'm not sure I'm familiar with her."

"She was one of the hottest actresses in the industry in the 90s."

"I don't remember her from any of your movies."

"She mostly performed with women."

She arched an eyebrow and took another drag from her cigarette.

"So are you a fan?" he said.

"Of women?" she said.

"Of me?" he said.

"Parts of you," she said.

"Want to be a fan of all of me?"

"Maybe," she said. "Depends if the other parts are as impressive as the parts I know."

"They are as—" He was interrupted again, this time by two police officers.

"Vincenzo Longhorn?" one officer said.

"Sì?" he said in his fake Italian accent.

"Yes. I see you are Vincenzo Longhorn," the police officer said.

"Okay."

"You are under arrest for indecent exposure, disrupting a public assembly, and induced fainting."

"Induced fainting?" Vincenzo said, glancing at the woman with blue eyes.

She shrugged.

"Please place your hands behind your back," the police officer said.

Vincenzo handed his cigarette to the woman. As the police officers placed handcuffs on his wrists, he said, "Those are really long-lasting cigarettes." Then he said, "You wouldn't happen to have bail money on you, would you?"

"What's in it for me?" she said.

"Whatever you want, bella regazza."

"Tempting," she said.

As the police officers led him away, one officer began reciting, "You have the right to remain silent…"

Vincenzo said, "You guys really say this? I thought it was just on TV."

"I don't know," the police officer said with a shrug, "they do it on *Law and Order*, so I figured I should probably do it too."

Vincenzo turned around and called back to the woman with the blue eyes, "Hey, what's your name?"

"Trouble," the woman said, and she flicked away his cigarette.

Chapter 4

The blue-eyed woman stared out the diner window, the bell above the door calling her attention each time customers walked in. A pair of old women leaning on one another for support. A teenage couple scheming their chew-and-screw. A family of four with a young daughter and son. Some schmo whose eyes popped out like a cartoon character when he caught sight of her blue eyes and perfect form. And then, finally, Vincenzo himself. His eyes didn't pop out. They were cool and knowing, as if he'd already calculated the best way to remove every stitch of her clothing.

Her pressed, crooked smile beckoned him, and he answered, striding to her. He stopped at the table without sitting down. "Looks like Trouble," he said.

"You have no idea," she said.

"May I sit down?"

"Can you handle Trouble?"

"Invite me to sit and I'll tell you how."

"You didn't ask *mother may I.*"

"Mother, may I?"

"Depends on what you have to offer."

"You've seen what I have to offer."

"It seems I have seen it. As well as a church full of horned up Betties and one old biddy in need of a pacemaker."

"They liked what they saw."

"But it's not as valuable when everyone gets to see it. That's called inflation."

"Do you want to see true inflation?"

"Now we're talking. Have a seat."

One of the small children at the next booth, the boy, said, "Daddy, what's inflation?"

"It's a finance term," the father said.

Vincenzo sat down in the booth and said to her, "Thanks for bailing me out."

She said, "Didn't want you hanging yourself in prison with that thing between your legs."

"Wouldn't do that. Too much to live for."

"You making a comeback?" she said.

"I can put it on your back if you'd like," he said with a twinkle in his eye, like Santa offering his stocking stuffer.

She smirked. "Subtle, are we?"

"I'm not so subtle when I want something. Like aiming for your C7 vertebrae."

The kid in the next booth said, "Daddy, what's a seesome vertebrae?"

"It's something in your back," the father said quickly. "What do you want to order?"

"You going to be able to make that shot from jail?"

she said. "Or better yet, in jail? With your roomie, Ben Dover?"

"Daddy, who's Ben Dover?"

"Look at the menu. Do you want a burger?"

Vincenzo said, "I'm afraid Ben will be on his own. Perhaps you remember signing a waiver before coming to the show. Turns out them old biddies did too."

"Do you always require a waiver to be signed before coming?" she said.

"A waiver is required anytime my...*little friend* enters the picture."

"Your *little friend*? You mean your monster cock?"

"Daddy, what's a monster cock?" The little boy at the next table said.

"It's a large rooster. Stop listening in on their conversation. It's rude."

"Who's being rude?" the little boy's sister said. "Timmy is being rude? Or those people are?"

"The waitress will be here soon," the father said. "Do you want fries with your burger?"

The blue-eyed woman said, "Should I be signing a waiver now?"

"Depends on how much danger you can handle," Vincenzo said.

"Perhaps I'm not the one tempting danger."

"Is Danger your middle name, Trouble?"

"That's right, Trouble Danger Galore."

"I thought it was Pussy Galore."

"Only for some," she said.

"Daddy, what's pussy?"

"It's a cat. Where is that damn waitress?"

The waitress walked past the family, as the father called, "Um, miss?" but she stopped at the woman and the porn star's table.

"More coffee?" the waitress asked the woman.

"No, thank you," the woman said.

The waitress then looked at Vincenzo, paused and said, "You look familiar."

Vincenzo smirked and said, "Well, you might know me."

"Are you the guy that bounced the check in here a few weeks back?"

"No," Vincenzo said, darting his eyes away. "I'm an actor," he added.

"So's everyone around here," the waitress said. "Christ, I had a reading for a commercial this morning."

He grinned. "No. I'm, let's say, a special actor."

"What're you like retarded or something?"

Vincenzo winced. "Jesus…what…you can't say retarded."

"You just did," the waitress said.

"Daddy, what's retarded?"

"Um, miss, when you get a chance?"

Vincenzo said to the waitress, "Did you ever see Dirk Diggler? *Boogie Nights*?"

"Sounds really old," the waitress said.

"Mark Wahlberg?"

"Marky Mark? He's a homo."

Vincenzo winced again. "Jesus, you, like, keep saying really horrible things."

"Daddy, what's a homo?"

"Homo sapien; it means human. Miss, can we please order?"

The waitress said, "So you're Marky Mark? You look terrible."

"No...I'm not Marky Ma—I look terrible?" He looked at the woman with the blue eyes and shrugged as if looking for help.

The woman said, "Make sure she signs a waiver first."

Vincenzo said to the waitress, "No. I'm not Mark Wahlberg."

"Then why bring him up?"

"Because his character in *Boogie Nights*, Dirk Diggler, was based on me...granted, a lot of people thought it was based on John Holmes, due to it being set in the nineteen seventies, but it was actually based on me."

"I've heard of John Holmes," the waitress said. "Guy with the really big dick, right?"

"Daddy, is a dick like a pee-pee?"

"Miss, please...?"

"Mine's bigger," Vincenzo said.

"I've heard that more than once," the waitress said.

Vincenzo looked pleadingly at the woman across from him again.

"I'd keep it in at the moment," the woman said.

"Want anything?" the waitress said to Vincenzo.

"Huh?"

"Do you want to order anything?"

"Jesus, I forgot that's what we were even doing here," Vincenzo said. "No thanks, I'm fine."

"I'd like to order," the father said, raising his finger.

The waitress said to the woman and Vincenzo, "So, no on the coffee and nothing for the retarded homo."

"Jesus," Vincenzo said, "you can't say these things."

The waitress shrugged and moved on to the next table. The mother of the two children said to the waitress, "That man at the next booth is vile."

"Tell me about it," the waitress said. "Kept talking about retards and homos."

"To think people still use language like that," the mother said.

"What's a retarded homo?" the little girl at the table said.

"I don't know," the waitress said, shrugging. "Ask that guy."

Vincenzo looked at the woman across from him and held up his hands.

The blue-eyed woman arched her eyebrow and said, "We were talking about your huge cock and my pussy galore."

"See?" the mother at the next table said. "He keeps saying filth."

"Well he is retarded," the waitress said.

"I didn't even say it," Vincenzo said, turning in his seat.

"You were just saying pussies and cocks in front of my children."

"I did hear pussies and cocks," the waitress said.

"Pussies and cocks," the little boy said.

"I'm literally the only one not saying pussies and cocks," he said.

"See? He said it again," the mother said, and she began to cry.

The father stood up. "I think I might need to teach this guy a lesson."

"What're pussies and cocks?" the little girl asked the waitress.

"Ask him," the waitress said, nodding toward Vincenzo.

Vincenzo stood with his hands up. "Look I—" As he stood, the little girl came around the corner of the booth and ran into him. Knocked to the ground, she looked up at what she'd just run into. When she spotted what she thought was a coiled snake in his pants, she began screeching like a police siren.

Vincenzo looked over his shoulder at the woman with the blue eyes. "You wouldn't happen to have more bail money, would you?"

Chapter 5

She stood in front of the diner, her delicate fingers holding a cigarette in front of her face, her free hand resting in the crook of her bent elbow. She squinted against the glare of a setting sun, its flare igniting her white shirt and beige skirt with the luminous halos of fallen angels.

Vincenzo burst out of the diner.

A burly oaf in a white apron was on his tail.

"And don't come back, you, you, malaka…you… big malaka," the oaf shouted in a fast, heavily accented stream of words.

When a safe distance away, Vincenzo waved at the oaf and stood beside the woman. She handed him her cigarette. He took a drag and said, "I can see why they named you Trouble."

"Hey, I'm not the one sticking my dick into every situation."

"There's only one type of trouble I want to insert my dick into."

The woman smirked. "Subtle as usual."

"Although I'm beginning to think trouble begets trouble."

She took back her cigarette, took a drag. "C'mon," the woman said, glancing over at the diner's front door and the oaf still eyeing them. She blew the smoke to the side and flicked her cigarette to the ground.

"I call police, you malaka, you big pig," the man shouted.

"How did you get out of there?" the woman asked him as she pulled him down the street.

"I had to apologize for being a misogynistic, homophobic, disabled-hating, pedophile groomer."

"Sounds like you got off easy."

"And pay them a hundred bucks to cover their ruined meal."

"I got my coffee for free," the blue-eyed woman said with a shrug.

"Where are we going?" he asked her.

"Looks to be a nice evening, let's go this way," she said, pulling him down an alleyway.

In the alley, their footfalls echoed like the ticking of synchronized heartbeats. The shadows danced with the splashes of dying light upon the stone way.

"Given I'm giving up trouble," Vincenzo said, "can I finally get your real name?"

"But Trouble likes you so much," she said.

"I think maybe I'd rather call you something else," he said.

"A rose by any other name…."

"Might not be trouble," he said.

"Vivian Petite," she said.

"Peddit?"

"P-E-T-I-T-E."

"Petite, like small?"

"Yes, but it's pronounced Petit."

"Why?"

"You'd have to ask my husband; it's his name."

"Husband?"

They stopped walking. She turned to face him. "Is that a problem?" she said.

"Depends."

"Worried he's bigger than you?"

"I suppose it depends on which parts are bigger than me."

"There is nothing big about my husband. He's small in every way," she said. She turned suddenly and strode away from him.

"Hey, hold up," he said.

She exited the alley, crossed a street without pausing at the curb, and was swallowed into the adjacent alley.

He stopped at the curb, glanced both ways, spotting the last of the sun glinting off car metal in the distance. He trotted across the street and into the far alleyway.

"Vivian, hey."

She continued to stride away, her echoing footfalls now like gunfire.

"Hey, wait," he said. Synchronizing his gait with her, he caught up with her and grabbed her arm, spinning her around to face him.

She shut her eyes and turned her head away.

"Hey…are you crying?"

"Don't look at me," she said, covering her face. "I don't want you to see me like this."

"Like what? Sad?"

"I must look terrible," she said.

"Well, I mean, you look sad. What's wrong with looking sad?"

"I can see you think I look ugly."

"No, I mean, you look exactly the same, just…you know, sad."

"I can see it in your eyes, you think less of me now."

"No, that might be…confusion? I don't know what you're seeing in my eyes. You're still, like, super hot, but I'm concerned, and maybe a little shocked?"

"That I look this horrible and pathetic?"

"No. It's just like the crying came out of nowhere and, frankly, you didn't seem like you'd ever be capable of crying. You know, because you seemed, like, so tough and all. Just out of character, and seemed, I don't know…really dramatic? Not like in a drama queen way, just, you know, a what the fuck is going on kinda way…" He cocked his head. "Do you hear, like, music or something?" He glanced up at the open windows. "Like a trumpet or something?"

She faced him again and grabbed him by the elbows, bringing her face close to his.

He still regarded the windows. "Like jazz or something?" he said.

She grabbed his chin and turned his face to hers. "You're so kind," she said.

"Well, I try to be," he said, his eyes rising toward the windows again. "It's like—" he paused, cocking his head to listen more closely "—a trumpet; you don't hear that?"

"Is all of you this kind?" She moved closer to him, her hips hovering within reach of his member.

"Um…okay, see? This is kind of a confusing shift again," he said, his Italian accent now completely gone. "And you seriously don't hear like a trumpet or something?"

She pointed up in the direction of a window above them and said, "Must be practicing."

Vincenzo looked up again and saw the golden glint of a trumpet in one of the third-floor windows.

"Is his instrument as impressive as yours?" she asked.

"Only if," he said, his accent returning, "the beautiful music you want to hear is the sound of pounding—"

The music stopped after what sounded like an elephant call.

"Wait, heads up," Vincenzo said, guiding her out of the way as something dropped from the window.

The object ricocheted off the ground with a clang and bounced up, catching Vincenzo in the crotch.

He dropped to his knees with an, "Oomph."

"Are you all right?" she said, placing her hands on his shoulders as he regained his breath.

"What is that thing," he wheezed, "a hand grenade?"

The object had landed a few feet from him and looked, in the dimming light, like a Nazi-era hand grenade.

"Excuse me," a soft nasally voice came from above them. "Excuse me. Can you toss my mute back up here?"

She helped Vincenzo to his feet, and they looked up to see a boyish-looking man with owl eyes peering down at them. "My mute," the man said, "I need it. Can you toss it up here, please."

Vincenzo wheezed and called up to the man, "I'm all right, thank you."

"You're welcome," the young man said. "Can I have my mute please?"

With slithering hips, the woman slid to the mute and, returning to the spot below the window, threw a perfect strike three floors above them.

The young man fumbled the catch and the object fell, ricocheting off the ground again. The woman pushed Vincenzo out of the way, as the thing would have hit his crotch again, and she caught it on the rebound.

"Eye on the ball, slick," the woman said and threw another strike.

This time the young man caught it and disappeared back into the window, leaving a disembodied, "Thank you," in his wake.

"Nice throw," Vincenzo said, awed.

"I played softball," she said.

"How the hell did that thing bounce like that?" Vincenzo said. "Was it made of rubber or something?"

The woman shook her head and shrugged. "I guess your crotch is just a magnet for trouble. Speaking of which, is it all right?"

"I don't know, to be honest." He hunched over, cupping his balls.

The trumpet began playing again as she sidled up to him. "Does it need some tender loving care?"

"You want to kiss it better?"

"Perhaps."

"Perhaps? Do you want to—? Seriously, I think it might be cut or something." He shifted his legs.

"Is it bleeding?"

"I don't know." He reached into his pants and then inspected his fingers. "Hold on," he said.

He shuffled to the side of the alleyway with his back to her and unzipped his pants. He pulled the beast from its lair and inspected it for cuts or bruises, allowing it to expand to its massive fourteen inches. A sudden flash of light caught his attention and, past his cock, he could see a light had popped on in one of the building's low, basement level windows. The face of a wide-eyed elderly woman now stared up at his outstretched member. Those wide eyes rolled to white and she dropped to her kitchen floor.

"Jesus Christ," Vivian said. "Two old ladies in one day."

Chapter 6

Vivian stood on the corner, looking out over the bay and the constellation of lights spattering its far shores. The lights on the bridge winked like the three men who'd already stopped their cars at the curb, assuming she was a pro. She flicked her lit cigarette into the lap of the last one.

Vincenzo and a policeman emerged from the alleyway.

Vivian stepped back into the shadows as another car approached her, but the man in the car drove away when spotting the cop.

"Thanks again, officer," Vincenzo said as he and the cop parted ways.

"You bet, Longhorn," the cop said. "You stay out of trouble now." He then chuckled and walked back into the alley toward the squad car on the far end, the car's flashing lights throwing flickers of blue across the alley's walls.

Vivian stepped out of the shadows and said, "I hope you've made your regular contribution to the Benevolent Policeman Association."

"Turns out he recognized me," Vincenzo said. "He was a good shit. We had a laugh about the whole thing. Although it was hard to convince him that a trumpet mute would bounce like that."

"So that was it? He just let you go?"

"Well, that and I had to let him take a picture of my dick."

"For evidence?"

"Nah. Dudes just like pictures of my dick. It's like getting a shot of some rare bird or something. A pic of a giant dick like that on their phone shows they're lucky."

"Or repressed homosexuals."

"Comes with the territory," Vincenzo said with a shrug. "If you have a freakishly large dick…."

"Then expect to be treated like a freak?"

"Then expect 'show us your dick' chants from a church full of women."

She looked away toward the winking lights of the bridge.

Vincenzo said, "And I could have used some backup there." He jammed his thumb toward the alleyway. "You know, someone to explain what had happened. A witness."

"I can't get involved. I…."

"Would just rather see me in the clink again?"

"I already bailed you out once."

"Yeah, and took off."

"I can't have my name in a police report. My…."

"Your what? Then you'd have to admit to yourself you've been slumming with a guy like me?"

"No. My…my—"

"Your what?"

"My husband will kill me," she said and stormed off across the street to the soundtrack of blaring horns.

Vincenzo followed her, negotiating the traffic in a trot. When he caught up to her, he synchronized to her stride. He could see she'd been crying again.

He said, "You know, for someone trying to avoid the police, you sure do a lot of jaywalking."

She chuckled through her tears and said, "It's legal now."

"Maybe you should have told those cars that."

She chuckled again, and her stride became a stroll.

They walked for a while toward the bay, toward the bridge crossing the black abyss of night.

He said, "So, your husband. Is this like: I'm late for dinner, my husband is going to kill me?"

"We have no dinner plans."

"So it's like: if he knew I was talking to you, he would kill me? Because I've heard that one before."

She slowly shook her head.

"So he's literally going to kill you?"

"If I don't go along with his wishes."

"He's, like, abusive? He beats you?"

"No."

"He's verbally abusive?"

"No."

"Does he make you think the flickering lights in the house are from the ghost of his dead, vindictive first wife?"

"No," she said, shaking her head. "He…makes me do things."

"Like sex things?"

"No."

"I guess I'm confused."

She turned on him and said, "He tries to make me the wife he wants me to be." She walked off again.

"Isn't that like…marriage?" Vincenzo said, following her.

They stopped at the wrought iron barrier along the water.

She said, "You've never heard of Herman Petite?"

"Why would I have heard of Herman Petite?"

"I figured in your industry, his name would carry some significance."

"He talent?"

"God, no."

"Producer?"

"No."

"Director?"

"Nothing that direct."

"Then what is he?"

"Plastic surgeon."

"Never heard of him," Vincenzo said. "But that doesn't surprise me. Most of the girls going under the knife don't talk about it. They would just disappear for a few days. We'd assume it was to drug rehab until they got back and suddenly their tits didn't jiggle as much during a pounding."

"You can certainly paint a picture with words," she said.

He shrugged. "I don't get paid to be a poet."

"You've never gone under the knife yourself?"

He shook his head. "Why? Not like anyone cares what the men's *faces* look like."

"Cops don't ask you to smile when snapping your picture?"

"That's right," Vincenzo said, looking out over the water. He then said, "So you're married to a plastic surgeon. Must be nice. Oodles of money and a touch-up anytime you want?"

"Not when the touch-ups aren't requested."

"He cuts you without permission?"

"I didn't say that. Pressure is the more accurate word. He pressures me into it."

"Your face is so perfect. Hard to believe that wasn't an act of God."

"My face is not his focus."

"Those tits are miraculous. He must be the Michelangelo of surgeons."

"He's never felt the need to fix my tits."

"Then what? Not the ass? If that ass isn't real, then I just found out there is no Santa Claus again."

"Huh? No."

"Then what?"

"Let's just say he's a very small man," she said.

"So, what, did he make you shorter somehow? Like take off part of your legs? Because that's weird."

"No," she said, shaking her head and scrunching her nose. "Parts of my legs? Seriously?"

"You said he's small."

"He's small," she said, "the same way you are large." She held up her fingers about an inch apart, as if recounting the world's worst fish story. "Do you get it now?"

"Oh…yeah," he said, nodding sympathetically—but to whom the sympathy was directed, he wasn't sure. "I get it. He has a little buddy?"

"If what you mean by a little buddy is that he has an itty, bitty dick, then yes."

"How small we talking?"

"If it were on the end of a hook, a fish would pass it by."

Vincenzo winced, still unsure as to where his sympathies should lie. He then said, "So what does this have to do with plastic surgery on you?"

"His dick is so small, he doesn't get the same sensation during sex as a typical man." she said.

"Okay…and?" Vincenzo said. "I still don't get what that has to do with you."

"His dick is *really* small, so…" she said, waving her hand in a prompting gesture.

"So…*how small is it*?" he said in the tone of the popular joke prompt.

"No," she said, waving her hand again. "It's so small that he has to…"

"Oh…yeah," Vincenzo said, "So he…nope, still don't get it."

"He still wants to have vaginal intercourse," she said, waving her hand once more.

"Oh…"

"So you get it?" she said.

"Yeah," he said with a shrug. "So he…nope, still not getting it."

"He performs a weekly labiaplasty on me."

"You thought that word would clear it up for me?"

"He tightens my labia minora to a snare drum."

"Your…?"

"Pussy."

"I was going to guess that."

"He's got it so tight, I can't even slip a digit in there," she said.

"How do you pee?"

"Seriously?"

"Yeah. Isn't that where it comes out?"

"You've literally fucked thousands of vaginas, and you don't know how they work?"

"I fuck them, not study them. Do I look like a gynecologist?" Vincenzo said.

"I can still pee fine," she said.

Vincenzo said, "If he likes it tight, why not just try anal?"

"Not tight enough," she said. "And not like he can

tighten that."

"Because something does come out of there, right?" Vincenzo said.

She offered only an epistemic shrug in response.

Vincenzo said, "Why doesn't he just fix himself? Why not enlarge his penis?"

"He claims it might change his sensation."

"Your husband sounds like a little prick."

A drum's rimshot rang out.

They turned and found a pair of street performers.

"Sorry," the drummer said.

"We're setting up here; didn't mean to interrupt," the saxophonist said.

Vincenzo looked up and down the nearly empty walkway. "Right here?" he said.

"It's our lucky spot," the saxophonist said.

"Best view of the bridge," the drummer added.

"We know it's the best view," Vincenzo said. "That's why we were standing here."

"Any requests?" the saxophonist said.

"To leave?" Vincenzo said.

"Sorry," the drummer said. "We're already set up."

"How about a song?" the saxophonist said.

"Anything but jazz," Vincenzo said.

"That's all we play," the saxophonist said.

"You don't have a mute on that thing, do you?" Vivian said, nodding toward the saxophone.

"No," the saxophonist said.

"I think it's safe," she said to Vincenzo.

Vincenzo said to the street performers, "Know any cool movie songs?"

"You got it," the saxophonist said.

Vincenzo and Vivian strolled along the wrought iron fence as the street performers began playing the theme song to *Taxi Driver*.

"Is this a cool movie song?" Vivian said.

"I have no idea," Vincenzo said. "Sounds boring. Movie probably sucks."

"You only know soundtracks featuring heavy seventies funk for when the pizza delivery guy stumbles onto a lesbian pillow fight?"

"You've done your homework," Vincenzo said. "You just described the plot of *Pussy Pillow Party*."

"You might call me a connoisseur," she said.

"Of pizza or pussies?"

"Of your films."

They stopped walking and faced one another.

"Must be hard," he said, "watching those films, when all you've got is your husband's…." He shrugged, unsure how to finish the sentence.

"Micro-penis?"

"Is that what it's called? It's really micro?"

"There are women with bigger clitorises," she said.

"Why not just leave him? Take half his loot and head off to Costa Rica or something?"

"Prenup," she said. "Steel tight. If I leave him, I get nothing. And…and he'll find me. He always does."

"You've tried leaving before?"

"Of course I have."

"How did you convince him to let you come to my sex seminar?"

"He thinks I'm at a tennis camp. I just needed to get out. Get out to…" She stepped closer to him. "To meet you. Your movies are what have gotten me through it all." She grabbed his hands, pulling him closer. "Thinking of your gentle touch and rough thrusts. It's all like a dream."

"It doesn't have to be a dream."

The street performers segued into the theme from *Body Heat*.

"It does," she said, looking away from him. She looked off toward the bridge. The twinkling distant lights dancing in her eyes. "With his weekly checkups, he'd know if I'm with another man."

"There are other ways to please a woman," Vincenzo said. "Ones I happen to have experience with."

"No," she said in a breathy sigh, turning her head and closing her eyes. "I…I wouldn't be able to resist you. I wouldn't be able to resist having you inside me."

"Wow, that was really direct. And graphic. I'm kind of getting a chubby right now."

Vivian moved to the wrought iron barrier, gripping the bars and looking out over the bay. "I don't know what to do." The lights glinted in her misty eyes.

"You can't reason with him?" Vincenzo said.

"Does he sound like a man who can be reasoned with?"

"I don't know," Vincenzo said with a shrug. "I've never met the guy."

"He's a man insecure of his manliness."

"Shit, yeah, okay, I know the type. He's a taint."

"A tate?"

"Taint. Small dick energy. Hell hath no fury like…"

"A man with a micro penis," Vivian said.

"Maybe he just needs a good talking to. Someone to let him know you're moving on."

"You?" she said.

"Could be. I can be convincing."

"He'd shoot you on the spot."

"I wouldn't go to your house to do it. Could be anywhere."

"He carries a gun everywhere. A .38 Special snub nose."

"Figures," Vincenzo said.

"Figures he'd carry a gun?"

"Figures a guy with a micro penis would have such a weak one. Doesn't matter. I can still give him a talking to."

"But what about his gun?"

"I'll bring a bigger one."

"Won't matter. There is no talking to him. He'll cut me out without a dime."

"Then maybe he needs more than just a talking to," Vincenzo said, looking out over the water as if spotting some answer on the distant horizon.

"Do you mean, like, beat him up? I told you, he'd cut me out and shoot you."

"Maybe more than a beating. Are you in his will, aside from the prenup?"

"Of course."

Vincenzo shrugged. "Accidents happen."

"Are you saying—?"

"No," he said. He glanced over his shoulder at the street performers. "I'm not saying anything. But accidents do happen."

"They do," she said in a breathy whisper. "But I don't know anyone who can help me."

"You might," he said. "How do I get in contact with you?"

She took a piece of paper and a pen from her purse. "You have to call this from a blocked number," she said, scribbling down a phone number. "He checks my phone. It needs to look like SPAM. Let it ring. If anyone answers, hang up. I'll call you back." She finished writing and handed him the paper and pen. "Give me your number."

He scribbled his number on the paper. Tore the paper down the middle, separating them, and handed his number and the pen back to her.

She lit a cigarette and turned to face the wrought iron barrier, again looking out over the bay.

He joined her, feeling the barrier's bars press against his body.

"I'll be free," she said in a pensive voice, blowing the smoke out over the bay.

"*We'll* be free," he said.

"Free to love," she said.

"Free to fuck," he said.

She glanced at him and said, "I can't wait to have you inside of my tight, yearning vagina." She tossed the cigarette over the barrier and into the bay. "We should be going," she said.

"Um…I'm going to need a few minutes," he said, still standing at the barrier. "It's stuck."

"What's stu—" She looked down and saw his hips pressed against the bars.

"It'll just be a few minutes," he said. "But maybe don't say anything else sexual."

She lit another cigarette and enjoyed the jazz music carried across the wind.

Chapter 7

Kraken McDavies tossed the gun onto the bed. "That's the biggest I could find," he said.

"I said the Dirty Harry gun," Vincenzo said.

"That is the Dirty Harry gun. It's a .44 Magnum."

"But Dirty Harry's gun was silver."

"No it wasn't. It was black."

"But that's not black."

"A second ago you wanted it silver. Now you want it black?"

"I want it like Dirty Harry's."

"It is. It's a .44 Magnum; gunmetal gray. If you want it like Dirty Harry's, then spray paint it black. Or silver. Or pink. I don't care. Why are you complaining? I told you I wasn't a gun dealer. You asked for a big fucking gun, and I got you a big fucking gun. If you asked for a particular drug, and I got something different, then you can complain, because I *am* a drug de—you know what, even then, don't complain. You know, you're pretty fucking particular. You know that? Remember that time you wanted an adrenal gland from a tiger, and I went into fucking Chinatown, only to find out one shouldn't fuck around with exotic animal traffickers in Chinatown? I almost got killed. Remember that?"

"Yes."

"Well I could have used this big fucking gun that day, and I wouldn't have cared what color the fucking thing was. Do you think I would have cared what color the fucking thing was?"

"No."

"That's right. No, I wouldn't have."

"But this is different," Vincenzo said with a shrug. "I need to look the part, because I want to—"

Kraken cut him off, saying, "I told you, I don't want to know what you're doing with this thing. I *did* want to know what you wanted the adrenal gland for, and I regretted asking. So now I don't want to know what you want this thing for. If you plan on robbing a bank with it, then don't tell me."

"I'm not robbing a bank. That's silly."

"Well if you plan on capping Howard Hosebager for ruining your career, then I don't want to hear that either."

"Howard and me are good now," Vincenzo said.

"Well if you plan on killing yourself, then I have an obligation to suggest you seek help. Otherwise, I don't want to hear it."

"I have no intention of offing myself."

"Well if you're scheming with some beautiful stranger to kill her overbearing husband and try to circumvent a rock-solid prenup, then keep it to yourself."

Vincenzo didn't say anything.

"Jesus, which part did I get right?"

"Pretty much all of it."

"God damnit," Kraken said, "I told you not to tell me."

"I didn't tell you," Vincenzo said. "*You* said it."

"But you weren't supposed to tell me I was right."

"I didn't. I didn't say anything. You told me not to say anything, so I didn't say anything."

"But by not saying anything, you ended up telling me."

"Just leave it as I didn't tell you anything," Vincenzo said, spreading his hands like an umpire calling a runner safe, "and leave it at that."

"But then I asked, and you confirmed it."

"That's right, *you* asked. See? I didn't say anything."

"All right, fine, we're just going to go back to me not knowing, and you not telling me anything," Kraken said.

"Okay. Deal. I won't tell you anything else." Vincenzo picked up the massive gun and hefted its weight.

Kraken said, "So is the wife in on it too, or are you going rogue or something?"

"Do you want me to tell you?"

"No."

"Then why ask?"

"Because I want to know."

"Then, yes. She and I are in on it together."

"Aw, man, I said don't tell me," Kraken whined.

"You said you wanted to know."

"Yeah, I said I wanted to know, but I also said don't tell me."

"Fine, then pretend I didn't tell you. Can we move on?" Vincenzo said.

"Okay. Yes. You didn't tell me anything. And I don't know anything," Kraken said.

Vincenzo inspected the gun. "Do you have the ammunition?" he asked.

"Shit, you need bullets too?"

"Of course I need bullets. How are Vivian and I supposed to murder her husband, Dr. Herman Petite, if I have no bullets?"

"For fuck's sake; why do you keep telling me more about this?" Kraken squealed.

"Okay, sorry. That one was on me. But, seriously, how could you forget the bullets?"

"When I sell someone smack, do I provide the needle?"

"If they ask for it you do."

"Well that's because I'm nice and believe it's important to be safe and curtail the spread of diseases. But if I sell coke, I don't provide the straw."

"Sure you do. You once gave me a rolled hundred-dollar-bill and told me to keep it."

"Well, I'm not a fucking gun dealer. I told you that."

"I do need bullets though," Vincenzo said.

"Then go out and buy some bullets."

"Don't I need, like, an ID or something to get the bullets?"

"Yes."

"I don't want to do that," Vincenzo said.

"Well, I can't go back to the guy I got the gun from and say"—Kraken imitated a dimwitted voice—"*oh, sorry, by the way, I need bullets too.*"

"Sure you can," Vincenzo said.

"No, I'll look like an idiot," Kraken said.

"Well, I'll look like an idiot when I'm behind bars because I bought bullets for a murder with my ID. I mean, come on, are you a gun dealer or not?"

"I've told you a million times, I'm not a fucking gun dealer."

"You didn't tell me a *million times*. That's impossible."

"Several times."

"Well, being a gun dealer could be a lucrative venture for you," Vincenzo said. "But I suggest, if you want a good reputation as one, you need to provide fucking bullets."

"Fine. I'll get you fucking bullets."

"Thank you."

"You're welcome."

Vincenzo inspected the gun again. "So where's the safety on this thing?"

"It's double action," Kraken said. "There is no safety."

"No safety?"

"Yeah. If you don't fuck around with it, it's safe enough. Just keep your finger off the trigger until you're ready to…do whatever it is you intend to do with it."

"Got ya."

"So, without telling me too much," Kraken said, "how long have you known this woman?"

"Little less than a week."

"Less than a week? Are you insane? How many of those days have you actually been face-to-face with her?"

"How many days, or how many times?"

"What's the difference?"

"Well it was a bunch of times on one day."

"Oh man," Kraken said, shaking his head. "How do you know she's legit? Have you at least tailed her?"

"Nah, her pussy's too tight."

"Huh? No, Jesus, not have you gotten tail from her; have you tailed her? Like followed her to see where she goes?"

"No, man. That's, like, stalkerish."

"No, it's smart. How do you even know she is who she says she is?" Kraken said. "Didn't you see *Chinatown*?"

"No. I don't like subtitles."

"Maybe you should hire a P.I. Or, better yet, did you even Google her?"

"I told you, her pussy's too tight."

"No. Google her, dipshit. Did you look her up on Google?"

"No."

"Jesus Christ. Go home and Google her. Then come back and I'll give you the gun and bullets only when I'm sure you're not going to blow your own head off for being duped."

"Deal." Vincenzo said. He stood up and put his hand out.

"What?" Kraken said.

"Aren't you going to give me the gun?"

"What did I just say?" Kraken said.

"I don't know. I was busy thinking about Googling that chick."

"And by Googling, you mean…?"

"Banging her."

"Go home and *look her up on the internet*." Kraken stressed these last words. "When you're sure about her, come back for the gun and bullets."

"Got ya."

They walked to Kraken's door and Vincenzo stepped out into the hallway.

"Hold on," Kraken said. "I can see in your eyes you're still thinking about banging that chick. What are you going to do right now?"

"I'm gonna go home and jerk off."

"Okay," Kraken sighed. "Let me know if you still need the bullets."

"I'm always loaded, baby, don't need bullets to jer—"

Kraken shut the door.

Chapter 8

After Vincenzo left Kraken's apartment, Kraken called him, his voice over the phone saying, "*Hey, dipshit, don't look up that chick on your own computer. Use the library or something.*"

"Why?"

"*Because you don't want any traceable connection to her.*"

"Then why would I use a public computer?"

"*Because they legally can't look at the searches of library computers. And you don't want anyone investigating your searches.*"

"Oh, because if I murder Vivian's husband, Herman Petite, then the cops—"

"*Jesus Christ, why do you keep—not on the cell phone. God.*" Kraken hung up.

Vincenzo walked down to the library and sat at one of the computers. After glancing over both his shoulders, he typed "Vivian Petite" into the search field.

On the library computer's screen, countless links for "petite" clothing "designed by Vivian" popped up.

"Jesus, is she a clothes designer?" Vincenzo muttered. "What is all this shit?"

He scrolled down.

More clothes. And more clothes. Clothes. Clothes. Dresses. Necklaces. Dresses. Sweaters. Dresses. Nail designs. More clothes.

Apparently there was a company called Designed by Vivian. Not to mention three major clothes designers with Vivian as a first name. And a jewelry designer. And what exactly was a nail designer?

He spotted a link for a Vivian Petite on Facebook.

He clicked on the link. A profile of a young Black woman with extravagant nails popped up.

"That must be the nail designer," he said under his breath. "Either that, or her husband is better at plastic surgery than I thought." He laughed.

"Do you mind?" a gruff voice said from behind him.

Vincenzo turned to find an old man hunched over one of the other computer screens.

"I'm trying to rub one out," the old man said. "And your yapping keeps distracting me."

"Rubbing one out?" Vincenzo said in disgust. "You can't do that."

"You never rubbed one out?" The old man said.

"Like five times a day," Vincenzo said. "But this is a library."

"Yeah, it's a library. So you need to be quiet. So if you don't mind…."

"You can't rub one out in a library."

"Of course you can. That's the beauty of public libraries. As long as you don't swear or expose yourself, you can do whatever you want."

"Really? Jesus," Vincenzo said. He glanced at the old man's computer screen. On it was a photo of the Olsen Twins from the days of their 1990s video empire. Vincenzo said, "Shit, dude, what are you doing?"

"What?"

"They're little girls."

"They aren't anymore."

"Yeah, but…dude, you can't rub it out to little girls."

"I told you, as long as I don't expose anything or swear, I can do whatever I want in a library."

"No. You can't rub it out to little girls anywhere."

"But they aren't little girls. They're way over eighteen now."

"But not in that picture."

"Doesn't matter. If I were rubbing one out to Raquel Welch, would that make it necrophilia?"

"If you were rubbing one out to a current picture of her, then yes."

"What you're saying don't make much sense," the old man said. "I like the Olsen Twins. So…."

"Why don't you rub one out to the current Olsen Twins then?"

"Kind of weird looking now," the old man said. He pouted out his lips like a duck and held his eyes wide with his fingers. "Now if you don't mind," the old man said, still holding his eyes open and pouting his lips, "I need to finish over here, so please be quiet."

"You too," Vincenzo said.

"Anything I want," the old man said, "as long as I don't swear or expose myself."

"I hope you rot in Hell," Vincenzo said.

"You too, sonny," the old man said. And they each turned back to their respective computer screens.

Vincenzo returned to the Facebook results and scrolled further down the list of profiles. No other "Vivian Petite."

"Shit," he said. "How—?"

"Shh," the old man said.

"Hey," Vincenzo said, turning toward the old man again. "I'm trying to search something, and a bunch of things keep popping up that I don't want."

"Happens all the time when searching porn," the old man said.

"No," Vincenzo said. "I mean—"

The old man said, "Kind of like when I search up little girls and all I get is midgets."

"Jesus, you can't say that."

"What? Midgets?"

"No searching for—well, yeah, the midget thing too. Jesus, maybe you just shouldn't talk."

"You're the one that asked," the old man said.

"I didn't ask about that. I asked about…look, I'm searching for a particular, real life person, whose name is similar to something unrelated. So I'm getting a million links to the wrong thing. Is there a way to, like, circumvent that?"

The old man said, "You're looking for what? Like circumvented dicks?"

"No. Jesus. It has nothing to do with porn. Look, let me put it this way: let's say you want the young Olsen Twins, and all that comes up is the current Olsen Twins."

"I would just search *young* Olsen Twins."

Vincenzo sighed. He said, "Thanks." Before turning back to his computer, he said to the old man, "Oh, and I hope you are castrated by a million rat bites in Hell."

"You're welcome," the old man said. "And you too. The rat bites, I mean."

Vincenzo returned to the blinking cursor on the screen. Typing "young Vivian Petite" wasn't going to work. He typed "Vivian Petite not dress."

All the links were for petite dresses again.

He typed "Vivian Petite not fashion."

Still all dresses.

He typed "Vivian Petite person."

Still all dresses and one link for an article about Vivian Leigh.

Vincenzo turned in his chair and called toward the old man, "Hey…."

"Did you try quotation marks in your search?" the old man said, not turning from his screen.

"Oh, no. Good idea," Vincenzo said. Before turning back to his computer, he said, "Thanks, you perverted piece of shit."

"You're welcome, you annoying pissant," the old man said.

Vincenzo turned back to his computer and tried his searches again, using quotation marks around the words "Vivian Petite."

Still dresses.

"Still not working," Vincenzo said to the old man.

"Don't know what to tell you, sonny."

Vincenzo said. "Let's say the most famous person in the world is someone named Olsen Young, and he just so happened to be a twin. And every time you searched for the young Olsen Twins, he showed up?"

"I would search for something related to the Olsen Twins, where they would possibly show up."

"So, instead of searching for the Olsen Twins, you'd search John Stamos and hope the twins showed up?" Vincenzo said.

The old man snapped, "They were like four on that show. Why would you want to search up the Olsen Twins as four-year-olds? You perverted piece of shit."

"No…I don't want to search the Olsen Twi—I'm just asking—"

"You need to get help, pal," the old man said, turning back to the poster of *It Takes Two* on his computer screen.

"You know, they *were* that age," Vincenzo said, nodding toward the movie poster. "On that Stamos show; they were that age too."

"Really?" the old man said, his voice raising a hopeful octave.

"Ugh," Vincenzo groaned. "I hope you die and have demons sew your dick into your mouth every day."

"Well, sonny, I hope they rip off your dick and fuck your new hole with it."

"Jesus, harsh," Vincenzo said. Before he turned back to his computer, he said, "And thanks for the help."

"Welcome."

Vincenzo turned back to the computer and typed "Herman Petite."

Countless links for dresses popped up again. Apparently there was a designer with the last name Herman.

Vincenzo took a deep breath and closed his eyes, holding the bridge of his nose. He then, combining all of the old man's advice, typed, in quotation marks, "'Dr. Herman Petite plastic surgeon.'"

Bingo.

Vincenzo stared at the photograph of Dr. Herman Petite, plastic surgeon. It was a Hollywood-style headshot with the man positioned, leaning back in a chair, shoulders turned one way, head facing toward the camera. His balding head looked too big for his body, a weather balloon hoping to break its mooring of a suit jacket and crisp white shirt. The smug look on the man's face made Vincenzo want to smash the screen with his fist.

Still no sign of Vivian.

He typed "Dr. Herman Petite, plastic surgeon, wife" into the search bar.

Up came links to different prominent movie stars and athletes and politicians, whose wives had work done by the "Augmenter General."

Vincenzo sighed, and typed "Herman and Vivian Petite" into the search field.

After scrolling through several more links to fashion, Herman found a link to a photo gallery of the "Best of the Bay Gala Ball."

He began muttering, "Best of the Bay Gala Ball," in tongue-twister style as he scrolled through the pictures, searching for Vivian.

Nothing.

Scrolling. Scrolling. He stopped. Some locked door of recognition suddenly turned its key. He scrolled back to a previous photograph.

There was Herman Petite and his helium head walking down red-carpeted stairs. And on his arm was a beautiful woman. Dark hair. And smoldering, dark, doe eyes.

Vincenzo read the caption beneath the photograph. "*Dr. Herman Petite and his wife, Vivian.*"

Vincenzo bellowed, "Aw, *fuck.*"

The smug face of the doctor's head seemed to be mocking him, but Vincenzo ignored it, squinting to focus on the woman in the picture. Could it be her, just with dark hair? He didn't know. But the dark eyes? Could she—

"Excuse me, sir? Sir?" a woman said.

Vincenzo turned to find an older woman peering over glasses at him.

"Sir?" she said.

"Huh?"

"I'm afraid I have to ask you to leave the library."

"Huh?"

"Your language. It's offensive to the other patrons. There are children here."

Vincenzo glanced at the back of the old man. His right arm was working vigorously. A picture of the Olsen Twins from the later *Full House* years on the screen.

"Um, sorry?" Vincenzo said.

"It's a little late for sorry," the woman said. "We can't have our patrons exposed to that kind of behavior."

The old man's breathing increased, and a muted groan rose from his depths.

"Okay," Vincenzo said. He stood and left the library without incident, hearing the content groan of the old man's satisfaction on his way out.

Chapter 9

When Kraken opened his apartment door, Vincenzo, standing in the hallway, announced, "I need that illegal gun you got me, because now I'm going to murder Vivian Petite instead of her husband, Herman."

"Jesus Ch—what the fuck? Get in here," Kraken said, yanking Vincenzo in through the door. He popped his head out into the hallway to be sure it was empty and then closed the door.

"Now I'm going to kill *her*," Vincenzo said.

"Whoa, slow down. What have you got me involved in now?"

"*You* involved? You're not involved."

"I *will* be. Somehow. I always end up involved in your stupid shit one way or another."

"Not this time. I swear," Vincenzo said.

"What happened?" Kraken said.

"I did what you said and Googled her and—by the way, weren't you looking for a nice necklace for your mom? Because there's this company called Jewelry by Viv—"

"Vincenzo, focus."

"Huh?"

"You were telling me about how you now want to murder some woman, remember?"

"Oh, yeah. I looked her up and found nothing. Just some dresses and jewelry that your mom might— never mind. So I looked up her husband. And she's not her husband's wife."

"What does that mean? They aren't married?"

"No. They are married, but she's not."

"I know you think you're making sense," Kraken said, "but try again."

"There was a picture of Dr. Herman Petite with his wife, Vivian. But the wife looks nothing like his wife."

"Believe it or not, I think I understand."

"It looked like a completely different chick," Vincenzo said.

"Well he is a plastic surgery guy…" Kraken said.

"That would be a pretty ridiculous twist if he'd changed her looks *that* much. And I'm not dumb enough to buy it."

"Then it sounds like you got Chinatowned."

"What's this got to do with tiger adrenal glands?"

"Not *our* Chinatown," Kraken said. "The movie *Chinatown*."

"You keep bringing that up. I have no idea what you're talking about."

"Okay. Remember in *Dick Me, My Darling* when Gina Parks is slapping Trudi Welles, and Trudi keeps saying 'I'm your sister, I'm your lover, I'm your sister, I'm your lover?'"

"Of course."

"Well, that's *Chinatown*."

"I'm so confused."

"Look; in the movie *Chinatown*, a woman hires a dick to tail her husband."

"So it's, like, gay porn?"

"No. Focus. Turns out the woman wasn't even the guy's wife. The dick had been set up."

"Does the dick at least get to fuck the woman?"

"For fuck's sake. Will you listen?"

"I am."

Kraken cupped his hands around his mouth like a megaphone, and said, "You're being had."

"Had?"

"And not in the good sex way. She's playing you."

"But why?" Vincenzo said.

"How would I know? Maybe the doctor, this Petite guy, botched this woman's plastic surgery, and she wants revenge."

"Nothing botched on this chick. Although…."

"Although what?"

"She did say he tightened her pussy so she could no longer use it."

"What? Like she can't pee out of it?"

"No," Vincenzo said. "Don't you know anything about pussies?"

"Clearly not," Kraken said.

"Her pussy is so tight she can't fuck regular dudes. She said her"—Vincenzo made air-quotes—"'*husband*' did it because he had such a small dick."

Kraken burst into laughter. "How small is his dick?"

"She said like a worm."

Kraken laughed, saying, "What a loser."

"Right?" Kraken said, laughing. Then he stopped and said, "Wait. If she's not his wife then his dick thing might be a lie too."

"Yeah, probably," Kraken said. "But I hope not because that's hilarious."

"I don't know what's true and what isn't," Vincenzo said.

"Yeah. Shit, dude. You want my guess?"

"Yeah?"

"Chick wanted to tighten her pussy; the Petite guy botched it; she wants revenge because now she can't have sex because penises won't fit in her vag."

"So this is all a red snapper?" Vincenzo said.

"That's a really weird way of phrasing it. But yes."

"So what do I do?" Vincenzo said.

"You need to tail her," Kraken said.

"Now we're talking," Vincenzo said. "I've been wanting to—"

"Again. Follow her. Not get tail from her."

"God damnit."

"You got to stake out her house and follow her."

"I don't know where she lives. I don't even know who she is."

"Then you at least need to stake out the doctor guy and find out if she's really his wife."

"I don't know where *he* lives."

"You can find that shit on Google."

"Can you do it for me?"

"Why?"

"Because I don't think I'm allowed back into the library."

Chapter 10

Parked directly across the street from Herman and Vivian Petite's house, Vincenzo sat in his bright teal 1989 IROC Z-28, listening to "King of Wishful Thinking," which was blasting on his Alpine. He was on stakeout, and he pulled his baseball cap over the sunglasses covering his eyes, to avoid being noticed.

He couldn't really see Herman Petite's house with the stone wall surrounding the property, but he could catch glimpses of the front door through the wrought iron gate. There was movement. Two people exited the front door. A man and a woman. The man, although wearing a hat and sunglasses, was definitely Herman Petite—Vincenzo recognized the balloon-head floating in his Polo shirt's collar. The woman, however....

Vincenzo squinted—not wanting to remove his sunglasses and ruin his cover—but couldn't make out if the wife was the Vivian he knew or not. The woman wore big Jackie-O sunglasses, and her hair was tucked up into a white baseball cap.

All he really had to go on was the ass. There was only one ass like the woman with the blue eyes's ass, and the one showcased under that short tennis dress now could well be it.

Vincenzo turned off the music, trying to hear voices, but their voices were more muted as they walked out of his view. Then there was the sudden, distant growl of a performance engine, and the wrought iron gate sliding open. A bright yellow Lamborghini Urus emerged from the gate and drove off down the road.

Vincenzo started his car, grumbling, "Figures he'd drive a Lambo. And not even a cool one." He fell in behind them.

He popped in the car's cigarette lighter and turned up the radio again. "Never Gonna Give You Up" was now playing, but it kept fading out with bad reception, the song being usurped by a nearby jazz station.

"What is this sh…."

The Lambo turned right at a green light. He was still several yards from the light when it turned yellow.

He sped up.

Then red.

"No," he groaned. He stopped at the light. "Shit." The lighter popped, and he lit his cigarette as the jazz still bled into his music. He hit the dashboard with his palm as if it were the music's fault the Lambo was now disappearing out of sight.

"Fuck it," he said, flicking the cigarette out the window and popping a waiting cassette into the Alpine.

"Danger Zone" broke out over the speakers, and Vincenzo gunned the engine, fishtailing as he took the right in pursuit of the Lambo. He avoided one honking car and passed another, but he couldn't see the Lambor—there it was, down another side street. He slammed on the brakes, almost getting rear-ended by a honking car swerving around him. He slammed the gearshift into reverse, shouting, "I got you now you dickless cunt." As he turned in his seat to check behind him, he noticed a small girl and her mother standing on the sidewalk. They stood beside his car, staring at him through his open passenger side window with slacked jaws.

"We can hear you, you know," the little girl said.

"Fuck, sorry," he said.

"We heard that too."

"Sorry," he shouted, backing the car up and taking off down the side street with squealing tires.

He'd lost sight of them again, but he had an idea where they were going.

He cut down another side road and shortcutted his way to what he thought to be their destination. He smashed the accelerator, cutting off an old lady in a car—who flipped him off—swerving around a stray dog, beeping at a kid about to run into the road to retrieve a wayward ball, and barely avoiding a fruit stand.

He saw the Lamborghini cross an intersection, and this time he made the light in enough time to turn in a couple of car lengths behind them.

"Bingo," Vincenzo said, as the Lambo pulled into the tennis club.

Instead of turning right to follow the Lamborghini, Vincenzo yanked the wheel left and pulled into a used car lot across from the club. He sat watching as the doctor waved off the valets and his wife exited the car with her racket. Without a word or gesture to his wife, the doctor sped out of the valet area, leaving the woman to saunter into the club. Vincenzo still couldn't tell if it was his Vivian or not.

Vincenzo got out of his car and trotted across the street. He strode through the hedged opening, past the fountain—where the cars circled to be taken by the valet attendants—and then up the stairs and into the club. His father had always told him that if ever he was in a place where he was not supposed to be, act like he belonged. And he was an actor after all. He—

"Can I help you, sir?" A woman dressed in a beige pantsuit asked.

"Huh?"

"Are you a member, sir?"

"Um…no? I'm Vincenzo Longhorn."

"Okay," the woman said. "Can I help you, Mr. Longhorn?"

"No thank you. I'm all set. Just browsing."

"Browsing, sir? Are you a guest of a member?"

"Um…no—shit—I mean yes?"

The woman twitched her head, and she said, "Whom are you a guest of, Mr. Longhorn?"

Two men, dressed in dark blue blazers, gathered behind him.

Vincenzo glanced at the men and said to the woman, "If I said a name would that help me right now?"

"Probably not," the woman said. "But if you want to give the name of a member, we'd be happy to deliver a message. As long as you were off the property when it was delivered."

Vincenzo glanced over his shoulders again and said, "Okay."

"Thank you, Mr. Longhorn," the woman said. "I hope you've enjoyed your browsing."

"I did, thank you," he said, and walked out of the building.

The hollow, distant thwaps of rackets against tennis balls were especially loud, and he craned his neck to see past the inner hedges, trying to see the tennis courts beyond. He saw the men in the blazers watching him from the club's doorway as he continued walking past the fountain toward the street, considering the hedges that encircled the property.

About to exit the hedge-line to the street, he stopped. Looking back to the club's doorway, he saw the men in the blazers were gone. He couldn't give up now. He needed to put an end to this speculation. Needed to go into secret-agent-mode and sneak back in there. He tried summoning the James Bond theme song into his head—something he did while filming one of his first films, *Pussy, Galore-ious Pussy*, where he played a British secret agent with an Italian accent that may or may not have sounded more Spanish. But all he could summon was the *Pink Panther* theme. Nope. Then the *Peter Gunn* theme. Shit. Then the *Mission Impossible* theme. Close enough.

He ducked back along the hedges surrounding the club, and eased his way along the perimeter of the property, keeping an eye on the front door for the men in the blue blazers. His steps were too frantic and dancing as he kept pace to the *Mission Impossible* theme in his head. He needed Bond's theme, the brisk steady striding beat of 007. How did it go again? It was like *Mission Impossible*, but…brisk and steady and stridi— there it was. The Bond theme rang out with sudden clarity. His pace became steady and determined as he headed past the valet shack, and toward the—

"Can I help you?" one of the valets said to him.

"Huh?"

"Are you a member, sir?"

"Um…."

Another valet attendant said, "Hey, that's Vincenzo Longhorn."

Another attendant arrived on scene, saying, "I think you're right."

"Hey, guys," Vincenzo said, holding up his hand.

"What're you doing here, Vincenzo?"

"I'm…uh…."

"Are you here to surprise one of these old biddies on her birthday?" One attendant said.

"Um…yes?"

"Must be Dorothy Alexander," an attendant said.

"Um…."

"Yeah, she seems like she'd be a Longhorn fan," another said.

"Uh…I…."

"Are you here for Dorothy?"

"Sure?" Vincenzo said.

"Who put you up to it?" an attendant said.

"Um…."

"Probably the King sisters and Mrs. Wellsley putting him up to it?" another attendant said.

"Uh…."

"Was it the King sisters and Mrs. Wellsley putting you up to it?"

"Uh, you bet?" Vincenzo said.

"So you're probably looking for a way to sneak in so they don't see you, right?"

"Yes?"

"Come on," one of the attendants said, waving his arm, "we can get you in through our back room."

"Can I get a pic of your dick?" another attendant said.

Vincenzo sighed and said, "Of course you can."

Chapter 11

Wearing a red blazer, a size too small for him, Vincenzo skulked out of the valet attendants' break room.

He mulled a moment around the outdoor patio, glancing at pasty white faces accentuated by gleaming white clothing—which, paired with designer sunglasses, seemed to be the same outfit for every single one of them, like some kind of uniform. He imagined every person seated there talking in a forced JFK affect.

He didn't see Vivian…

Or at least *his* Vivian…

Or at least the Vivian he saw getting into the Lamborghini…

Or at least he didn't see the woman he was looking for, which he didn't know he was looking for…no, that's not right…

This was so confusing.

Trying to call back the James Bond theme, he moved forward in a confident, yet furtive, stride, regarding each sneering snob with equal parts reverence and disdain. As he moved further into the circle of exclusivity, his confidence in pulling off the whole belonging vibe was waning. Then he heard a familiar voice say, "Excuse me, sir…?"

Vincenzo turned to find the woman in the beige pantsuit. The men in the blue blazers flanking her.

The woman said, "Mr. Longhorn, I presume?"

"Um…."

"Or is it…" she read the tag on his red blazer, "Jorge?"

"Um…no hablo the Americano?"

The woman twitched her head, and the men in the blue blazers stepped forward.

A woman's voice halted them, saying, "I'll deal with this."

Vincenzo immediately recognized the velvet voice, and he turned to find Vivian, *his* Vivian, dressed in the white tennis outfit and hat, and the same Jackie-O sunglasses he'd seen getting into the yellow Lamborghini. She took off the sunglasses, revealing those sparkling blue eyes, confirming her identity.

"Are you sure?" the woman in the beige pantsuit said to Vivian.

"Yes," Vivian said.

"You know him?" the woman in the beige pantsuit said with a sneer.

"I know *of* him," Vivian said. "Apparently the King sisters hired him to surprise Dorothy Alexander."

"That's right," Vincenzo said, "The Kane sisters hired me."

"King," Vivian said.

"The King sisters hired me."

"He's an exotic dancer."

The woman in the pantsuit arched her eyebrow regarding Vincenzo.

"Why don't you show them your moves, Mr. Longhorn," Vivian said.

"Now?"

"Yes."

Vincenzo glanced around before swinging his hips and accentuating the moves with a few pelvic thrusts (finding it difficult to dance to the James Bond theme, which was still playing in his head).

The two men in blazers snickered. The woman in the pantsuit raised her eyebrows again. She then held out her hand, palm up, saying, "I think that's good, Mr. Longhorn."

Vincenzo slapped her hand in a giving-five gesture, saying, "Thanks," as he continued to dance.

"No," the woman said. "I was holding out my hand for Jorge's jacket."

"Oh. Yeah," Vincenzo said, and with a few more pelvic thrusts, he stripped off the jacket and tossed it onto the woman's outstretched hand.

The woman turned and, shaking her head, walked away. The snickering men in blazers followed her.

When they were out of earshot, Vivian said, "Care to tell me what you're doing?"

"I'm dancing?"

"Why?"

"You told me to dance."

"And dance you did. Now tell me the *why* you're here part."

"Don't get all high and mighty with me, princess" Vincenzo said. "First, I have a few questions of my own."

"Does it have to do with why you're here?"

"Yes."

"Then, by all means, ask."

"Why aren't you who you said you are?"

"You might need to ask that one again."

"I did something called *Googling* you and your husband, and you're not his wife."

"I can assure you I am."

"You don't look like her."

"Need I remind you he's a plastic surgeon?"

"Woman I saw in the picture was a brunette."

"Hair dye."

"With brown eyes."

"Eye color can be changed."

"Aw, man, those beautiful blues are contacts?" Vincenzo whined.

"Nothing so temporary."

"You have fake eyes? How can you see?"

"Keratopigmentation."

"So, what, they're like cameras, or…?"

"Not fake eyes. It's pigmentation inserted into a corneal hole."

"Your butt?"

"My eye, Vincenzo. The cornea."

"Why didn't you tell me? You told me he only tightened your pussy too tight."

Her gaze shifted a moment to her feet. "I was too embarrassed to tell you the rest."

"But you weren't too embarrassed to tell me about the pussy part?"

She looked away, the sun glinting in her Keratopigmentated eyes. "I was worried that if you knew I'd been so physically altered, you wouldn't take me seriously enough to…." She shut her glinting eyes, unable to go on.

"To what?" Vincenzo said.

"To want me," she said.

"Seriously? You think some hair dye and ker-plunked eyes would chase me away?"

"I don't know. Will it?"

"No," Vincenzo said. "Of course not. I don't care what's original and what's—is your ass real?"

"Yes."

"Then, no. I don't care what's real. I just want you. The smoldering hot babe that is you."

They took a step toward each other, as if to embrace, but she suddenly stopped, as if being ripped away with great effort.

"Why do you keep pretending like you don't know me?" Vincenzo said.

"Because…" she said.

"Because…?"

"What we're planning to do? My husband?"

"Oh." He looked off at the tennis players a moment. "Because…?"

"People might have questions if my husband were to show up dead after I was seen embracing another man publicly."

"How did you know about the Kane sisters story?"

"King sisters?"

"How did you know about the King sisters story?"

"I asked Jorge what you were doing here."

"You know Jorge?" Vincenzo said. "That guy's great."

"I come here every day; why wouldn't I know Jorge?"

Vincenzo shrugged, "I don't know…rich people… the help…I don't know; seems like rich people wouldn't want to interact with them."

"I wasn't always rich, Vincenzo."

"Well how did you know I was even here to ask Jorge what I was doing here?"

"I saw you following us."

"Us, who?"

"My husband and me."

"Oh. Really? You saw me?"

"Vincenzo, *everyone* saw you following us."

"Did your husband notice?"

"Yes. Vincenzo, you took a couple of corners sideways and almost took out a fruit stand."

"But I *didn't* take out the fruit stand," Vincenzo pointed out.

"The almost was enough for my husband to notice."

"So is he suspicious?"

"No," Vivian said. "He just thinks it was some yahoo wanting to race his high-performance car."

Vincenzo scoffed. "High-performance. It was a Urus."

"You need to go."

"Why?"

"Because we can't be seen together for too long," Vivian said.

"When will I see you again?" he said.

"Soon," she said. "Unless you plan to tail me in the most gaudy vehicle possible again. Maybe a psychedelic hippy van next time? See if you can keep up with the Lamborghini in that? Or maybe you can get the Batmobile?"

"Believe me, I could keep up with a Urus in the van, don't you worry."

"The point is, *don't* keep up," she said. "Stop acting so suspicious. Not that you'll be able to follow me much, he doesn't let me out often. Only here."

"Then maybe I'll come back here."

"*Don't* come back here. I'll call you when I get the chance. Now, c'mon, you need to get out of here."

"But what about Dorothy and the Kane sisters? Shouldn't I give them their show?"

Vivian stared at him and said, "But Jorge made that…you get that the King sisters never actually hired you, right?"

"Of course. But I should still give them what they want, right?"

"There is no—"

A voice calling from the distance cut her off. "Excuse me, excuse me. Serving girl?"

Vincenzo and Vivian turned to find an older woman calling from the courts area. The woman's whites smeared with patterns of her bright red lipstick, her chicken wing arm's skin jiggling with her vigorous waves.

"Time to serve, serving girl," the woman called.

Vivian nodded her head in the woman's direction. "*That's* Dorothy Alexander," Vivian said. "She has dementia. She's a little out of it, and we don't need you putting any more old ladies into the hospital. Although…" Vivian stared a moment at the woman, "she might be more apt to put you in the ER."

"Why does she call you serving girl?"

"She thinks I'm her childhood maid. I must look like her or something."

"That must have been one super-hot maid," Vincenzo said. He then shifted his hips against the tightening in his already-tight pants. "I'm now envisioning you in a maid outfit, and it's really turning me on."

Vivian turned back to him, seductive, and stared into his eyes, saying, "You be a good boy, and you will get to see me in that maid outfit."

Vincenzo shifted his hips more vigorously and he readjusted the crotch of his pants, saying, "Shit, I should maybe get out of here."

"Good idea," Vivian said. "Wait for my call."

"Okay," Vincenzo said with a groan and darted away through the crowd, still adjusting his tightening pants.

Chapter 12

She didn't call that night. Vincenzo tried calling the number she'd given him, remembering to block his number. She didn't answer. And she didn't call him back like she'd said she would.

He spent the next day working out with his dumbbells and sitting around his apartment watching *Dick Me, My Darling* a couple of times. He made a few phone calls, putting out feelers for more sex seminars, but word had gotten out about the old woman incident. He'd wait a couple of weeks for word to become legend. Eventually, knocking out some old biddy with his oversized dick would become an asset.

He also tried calling Vivian again. Twice. But no answer.

That night he received a call. The caller ID said "Dr. Herman Petite Cosmetic Surgery."

He answered the phone tentatively. "Hello?"

"*Hey.*" It was Vivian, speaking in a breathless whisper.

"Hey. Are you all right?" He leaned back on his couch, his heart pounding in his chest. Feeling like being in high school again, talking to the girl he liked from math class. Feeling the need to twirl the ghost of an ancient receiver cord in his fingers.

"*I'm tired,*" she said, sounding more than tired. It was the deep exhaustion of someone on the verge of giving up.

"What is it?" Vincenzo said.

"*He gave me another impromptu procedure yesterday.*" There was a deep silence along the phone's static. He then realized she was crying. "*I can't take this much more.*"

"Where are you?" he said.

"*I'm calling from his home office.*" Silence again. "*I want to burn this fucking place down.*"

"Don't go all Lisa Left-eye on me," he said.

"*I don't know what that means.*"

"Really? TL—don't go chasing—never mind. There was this singer chick who burned down her boyfriend's house, and she ends up going to jail…or something like that. There are better plans. We *have* a better plan."

"*We don't* have *a plan at all,*" she said wearily.

"Well, I thought…I thought the plan was to…you know, kill him. Get you free."

"*That's an idea. Not a plan.*"

"Yeah, well…then what's the plan?"

"*That's what you were supposed to be working on. Did you get the gun?*"

"Yes and no."

"*Meaning?*"

"Meaning I procured a gun, but he won't give it to me yet."

"*What does that mean?*"

"Procured? I thought it meant to get something."

"*No. What does it mean that he won't give it to you?*"

"It means…it's complicated. But not too complicated that I can't get the gun."

"*So all that's left is to figure out when and where to do it.*"

"Well that's hard to figure out, given I'm not allowed to follow you."

"*You're not allowed to follow* me. *You can follow* him. *Wait, follow is the wrong word. It might be smart to observe him from a distance. And not in something that sticks out like a teal IROC. And not with Tears for Fears blasting out the window.*"

"It was Go West."

"*I miss you,*" she said suddenly in a breathless whisper.

"I miss you too."

"*Have you been thinking about me?*"

"Every second."

"*What are you going to do to me when you have me?*"

"I'm going to rip off your clothes."

"*Yeah?*"

"And fu—well, I probably can't do that right away, given your condition. So maybe start with some kind of planned progression of—"

"*I want to suck your giant cock.*"

"Oh…yeah, that works too."

"*I have to go. I think I'm falling in love with you, Vincenzo Longhorn.*"

"Really? Wow, that was pretty fast. But, yeah, cool. I'm falling for you too."

"*I'll call when I can.*"

"Oh, okay, cool. I—"

She hung up.

"Really? No goodbye?" He said to the silent phone line.

He glanced at the television, *Dick Me, My Darling* on the screen again. Gina Parks slapping Trudi Wells, reenacting a scene Vincenzo had only recently discovered was from *Chinatown*. Vincenzo winced watching it. He remembered that, at the director's request, Gina was really slapping Trudi. Vincenzo remembered how much it had shook the girls, both of them sobbing apologies and forgiveness to each other when it was done. It made the subsequent, requisite lesbian scene super hot, however, as the girls fell passionately on one another.

Vincenzo fast forwarded to the good part.

Chapter 13

Kraken answered the phone with one word. "*No.*"

"No, what?" Vincenzo said.

"*There is no what. Just a no. Whatever it is, the answer is no.*"

"But I haven't asked for anything yet."

"*Exactly. And please keep it that way. I know you are going to somehow directly involve me in whatever it is you're involved in. I am trying my hardest to avoid any kind of entanglement in this; whatever this might be. Is that clear enough?*"

"That was a very long explanation, when a simple no would suffice."

"*I did say no.*"

"But I'm not calling about anything like that."

"*Then what do you want?*"

"Just saying hi. How's your mom?"

"*My mom's good,*" Kraken said with a wary tone.

"Cool," Vincenzo said. There was an awkward silence, then Vincenzo said, "Hey, I need to borrow your car."

"*Aw, fuck,*" Kraken said.

This time, Vincenzo planned to keep a lower profile when tailing Petite. He cruised down the street in Kraken's bright orange EV Mustang. Kraken had N.W.A. on his sound system, and, with that sound system being far too complicated for Vincenzo to figure out, he went with it, bobbing his head along with the music, windows down, wind in his hair, until, waiting at a stoplight, he realized just how many N-words were erupting from the open windows.

He looked out to see a Black man staring at him with his eyebrows raised.

Vincenzo struggled to stop the music, but still couldn't figure out the sound system. He then said to the man on the side of the road, "This isn't my car."

The Black guy said with a shrug, "This isn't my street."

Vincenzo struggled with the radio again, saying, "I'm trying to stop the N-word."

"Welcome to the fight, my brother," the man said. "Light green."

"Light green? Like, it ain't easy being green?"

"No. Light *is* green." The man pointed at the stoplight.

"Oh, thanks." Vincenzo said and continued on his way.

He drove to the Petite's home again. This time parking a little down the street and waiting for the yellow Lamborghini to come out. The neighborhood was quiet—aside from the music blasting from Kraken's car. Except for a few landscaping trucks, there was very little traffic. As "Alwayz into Somethin'" ended, Vincenzo could hear the distant hum of mowers and a yapping dog. The picture of suburbia, Ward and June land, if Ward were abusing June, and June was about to off him.

The next song, "Just Don't Bite It," began playing on the radio—a girl's voice describing a blowjob, complete with slurping. Vincenzo was lost for a moment in the song, trying to discern, from his vast library of remembered blowjobs, just how accurate the sounds were. He felt the uncomfortable tightening in his pants again. The pressure becoming so great, he was tempted to unzip and release, but then a bright yellow Tesla popped out of the property's entrance, Petite's head bobbing in the window.

The next song was "Straight Outta Compton," and Vincenzo took off after the Tesla. He missed feeling the rumble of an engine beneath the music's bass line. Driving a silent, electric Mustang was like having his pecker soften during a money shot.

The Tesla stopped at a light, and Vincenzo tried to hang back long enough for another car to pull in before him—as to not be directly behind Petite—but no cars came. Vincenzo stopped a full car length away. He bent down, taking the time to try and change the music, or at least turn the volume down.

"Whatever happened to a simple knob?" he said.

When he looked up again, the Tesla was gone.

"Shit."

He drove forward. Then, suddenly noticing Petite had taken the right, Vincenzo swung the Mustang right in pursuit, mashing down on the pedal. The acceleration of the electric engine was otherworldly, and he felt a slight stiffening in his pants. "All right. Now we're talking," he said, squinting through his sunglasses to keep an eye on Petite.

The Tesla took another right.

Vincenzo followed. The Tesla picked up speed a little, and Vincenzo pressed down on the Mustang's pedal, this time trying to head off a line of merging cars before they pulled in front of him. He needed to keep his distance, but not that much distance. He couldn't get ahead of the other cars, so he pulled into the left lane. At the next light, he was forced to pull up beside Petite.

Vincenzo glanced to his right, trying to size up his quarry. He could see the man's balloon head bobbing in the car's interior. The man's own eyes, hidden beneath his sunglasses, stared straight ahead. The man's hands tightened on the steering wheel as the light turned green.

The Tesla turned right. Vincenzo looked up, seeing the green arrow in front of him, and realized he was in a left turn only lane.

"God damnit," he groaned, watching Petite's car shrinking out of sight as the cars behind him began beeping.

"Fuck it." His hands tightened on the steering wheel

as he maneuvered the car through the right lane of traffic. "Sorry," he called. "I'm sorry, I need to get that guy." The light turned green again, giving him the chance to make the turn, and he waved to the others in apology, and as a thank you for not shooting him. After all, people in this town have been shot for much less, like loving the wrong woman.

Wait…was this guy, Petite, going to get killed for loving the wrong woman…?

No, he would be killed for hurting the wrong woman.

Vincenzo's eyes narrowed, searching for the Tesla, and he spotted it, finding it in time to see Petite take another right.

"Where's this guy going?" he said under his breath.

He took the right and then saw the yellow Tesla turn right again.

"Are we…?" He pulled onto the road to see Petite drive past the Petites' house. "We're going in circles," Vincenzo said.

Vincenzo slowed to glance at the house's address to be sure. It was their address, and it was their house. When he looked up, he no longer saw Petite. Goosing the accelerator, and feeling the car jump in response, he pulled to the intersection in time to see the yellow Tesla had taken the right and was about to take another one. He swung the car right in pursuit.

"Where is this guy going?"

At the next right, he no longer saw the yellow car. He took the right, and then the next right. Still no Petite.

"Shit."

He approached Petite's home again. Slowing, he craned his neck to see if the car had maybe returned home, but the wall obscured most of the property. Leaving the house behind, he took the next right again, glancing down side streets and calculating whether he should go directly to Petite's office or maybe the tennis club.

When he looked in his rearview mirror, he saw the Tesla directly behind him.

"What the…?"

Perhaps it was a different Tesla, but then he saw Petite's bobbing, balloon head behind the Tesla's wheel.

Vincenzo stopped at a red light, trying to discern the intent of the man in the rearview mirror, the man whose eyes were hidden behind aviator sunglasses.

Vincenzo's hands tightened on the steering wheel.

The traffic light remained red.

Glancing in the rearview mirror, he noted the head and its blank expressionless sunglasses-hidden expression, as if someone had drawn sunglasses onto a helium balloon.

The traffic light was still red.

Vincenzo needed to play this one cool. Stay inconspicuous. Don't let on that he's intimidated, or that he even notices the guy behind him.

The light turned green, and Vincenzo gunned the accelerator, turning left. He expected a roar of an engine and a squeal of tires, but instead, the electric car silently launched into instant acceleration, cutting off the traffic coming from the other way.

So much for inconspicuous.

He rocketed down the street, screaming laughter as "100 Miles and Runnin'" began playing on the sound system. There was no way Dickless back there would be able to negotiate through the traffic coming from the other way. Vincenzo was home free. But when he glanced in the rearview mirror, the yellow Tesla was rapidly catching up.

He spotted a right turn up ahead. Taking his foot off the accelerator, he felt the car's instant deceleration. "Like a freaking downshift," he laughed. He took the right, and with the next burst of acceleration, he said, "I love this thing." But taking another left, he grumbled, "Needs fucking engine sounds though."

Looking up to the rearview, he saw the Tesla still behind him.

A left turn up ahead. He waited until the last second to make the turn, nearly missing the bumper of a car going in the opposite direction. "Tokyo Drift," he shouted, the Mustang's wheels bumping over the curb as he straightened the steering wheel, nearly hitting a fruit stand.

The Tesla missed the turn.

"Haha, motherfucker," he said.

He slowed, regarding the street signs. "Where the fuck am I?"

All the intersecting streets looked identical, but when he looked down their length, they seemed to impossibly bend and turn in different directions at their ends. "What is this place, a maze?" he murmured.

As he regarded the different paths, the yellow Tesla shot out from one of the side streets, stopping in front of him. Blocking him.

With the Tesla's driver-side window directly in front of him, Vincenzo now stared at Petite's profile until Petite calmly and slowly turned his head to face him. They silently regarded each other before Vincenzo put the Mustang in reverse and gunned the car backward down the street.

The Tesla turned in pursuit.

Vincenzo going in reverse, Petite going forward, the two men stared at one another through their windshields before Vincenzo turned the steering wheel hard, tapped the brake, then the accelerator again, straightening the steering wheel. The Mustang rotated 180 degrees in a perfectly executed J-turn.

Vincenzo blinked. "I can't believe I just did that." And he continued down the road, again screaming laughter.

The main road was up ahead, and he knew he could lose this guy in the traffic. "C'mon, let's play, motherfucker," he shouted. "Whoa." He almost hit the fruit stand again as he swung onto the main road, cutting off a garbage truck. "Haha, get around that, you tiny dick," he shouted toward the Tesla, which he could no longer see.

He slowed the Mustang, bringing the garbage truck close to his rear bumper, ensuring the Tesla would not be able to get behind him. The garbage truck driver, leaning over his steering wheel and flinging his hand in the air, was not pleased.

The Tesla, now in the left lane, darted past the garbage truck. When Petite noticed the Mustang, he matched Vincenzo's speed, to the exasperation of the cars behind him. Vincenzo and Petite jockeyed for the slowest position as other car-drivers cursed and beeped.

The garbage truck suddenly turned up a side road, creating a void in traffic, and the Tesla slid in to fill that vacuum.

"Okay, Pee Wee, nice move," Vincenzo said. "But watch this."

He spotted a red light ahead and a break in traffic from the opposite direction. He yanked the wheel, cutting off a beeping car about to pass him in the left lane. Straining to keep the wheel turned left, like a helmsman against piling seas, he made the turn down a side street, disappearing between two buildings.

"Fuck, yeah," he shouted, already swinging left into another turn, which was a dead end alley. "All right, motherfucker, watch me make this horsey disappear."

When Vincenzo put the Mustang in reverse, nothing happened. The music cut out. He sat in silence with his hands in the air, afraid to touch anything. "What the…?" Pressing buttons and sliding the shifter back and forth, he then spotted the empty battery icon blinking on the dashboard. "Fuck me," he groaned.

Abandoning ship, he popped out of the driver-side door. Heading toward the opening of the alleyway, he'd disappear into one of the stores, maybe even the diner he knew was around the corner with the great egg sand—he stopped as the yellow Tesla pulled in behind the Mustang.

Petite was out of the car immediately, brandishing a snub-nosed .38 Special.

"Whoa," Vincenzo said, raising his hands.

"Why are you following me?" Petite screamed. "Who are you?"

Waving his hands in front of him, Vincenzo said, "Wait, you—"

"Are you trying to rob me?"

Still waving his hands in front of him, Vincenzo said, "No, you—"

"Staking out my house?"

"No—"

"Is this a kidnapping attempt?"

"No—"

"Are you another federal investigator?"

"Huh?"

"Are you looking to fuck my beautiful wife?"

Vincenzo stopped waving his hands and paused a moment before saying, "Look, will you listen to me?"

"What? What is it?"

"Your car is on fire," Vincenzo said.

Petite turned around to find his yellow Tesla engulfed in flames. "Jesus Christ," he screamed.

Chapter 14

Vincenzo returned from around the corner of the alleyway and handed Petite one of two wrapped egg sandwiches and a coffee. Vincenzo then sat beside Petite on the curb, and the two opened their egg sandwiches. As the fire trucks cleared out, the flatbed moved in to collect the charred husk of the Tesla.

Petite swallowed his bite of food, and then a sly grin spread across his face. The grin of a Cheshire Cat across the moon face of his bulbous head. He held up the sandwich, saying, "You weren't lying, Vincent, these are amazing."

"Actually it's Vincenzo."

"Sorry," Petite mumbled through a mouthful of sandwich. He swallowed and said, "Where did you get these things?"

"McDonald's," Vincenzo said, taking a bite of his own sandwich.

"Fuck you," Petite squeaked.

Vincenzo chuckled, almost choking on his food. He swallowed it and said, "They're from a small family diner around the corner. Been there a few times. Folks are nice." He took a sip of his coffee, and then used the cup to gesture into the distance. "You got me a little lost up in the neighborhoods there, but once I got back on the main road, I knew exactly where I was."

"Except for this dead end here," Petite said, nodding toward the Mustang.

"Apparently." Vincenzo then nodded toward the Tesla being loaded onto the flatbed. "You're surprisingly calm about all of this…" he said, sipping his coffee, and then added, "now."

Petite grimaced, and then his sly smile returned. "As opposed to when I was waving my gat in your face?"

"Could that thing really be called a gat?" Vincenzo said.

Petite shrugged. "Got you quivering." He laughed and shrugged again. "Anyway, I got it out of my system. And as far as the car goes…looks like the world's richest man will be buying me the McLaren I've wanted, and then some, after I sue his ass."

"I guess if you're going to act like Steve McQueen, then you should stick with the Mustang," Vincenzo said, motioning toward the Mach E.

"McQueen would have remembered to charge it before he left the house," Petite said.

"Fair point."

"So, you need to explain this all to me again," Petite said. "Why the hell have you been following me? Something about your mother needing life-saving surgery?"

"She has skin cancer, and needs it removed," Vincenzo said.

"That would be a dermatologist," Petite said.

"And breast cancer," Vincenzo added. "She needs her boobs taken off."

"That would be an oncologist"

"And her feet don't work right; she can't walk."

"Podiatrist."

"She wants to be a man?"

"Huh? Yeah, I can do that, but she needs…how old is she…? Never mind. Why didn't you just call my office?"

"That's a really good question. I guess…I was embarrassed?"

"Embarrassed about which part?"

Vincenzo watched the Tesla being loaded onto the flatbed, sighed, and said, "Look. I haven't been completely honest with you. Truth is…my dick is too big, and I think I might want to make it more normal."

"How big is your dick?"

"Fourteen inches."

"Fuck you," Petite squeaked. He cleared his throat, and in a more doctorly voice, said, "Oh, really? Fourteen inches you say?"

"Yeah. And it's become a real hindrance."

"Of course," the doctor nodded. He ate the last of his sandwich and after swallowing it, he said, "How, exactly?"

"Huh?"

"How is a fourteen inch dick a hindrance?"

"Well, for one thing, it's incredibly uncomfortable …you know, when I get an erection while wearing pants. Kind of like, you know when the hulk outgrows his clothing?"

"Why not wear sweatpants or something?"

"Because then people can see it. Thing points out like I have a pennant sticking outa my crotch. At least tight pants act as a kind of girdle or something. And frankly, it takes so much blood to fill the thing, my brain gets foggy and I get dizzy. Kinda, you know, makes me stupid."

"You're still getting random erections at your age?"

"Yeah." Vincenzo shrugged. "It's like Pavlov's Dog or something. All the years I spent needing to get hard on cue has made the slightest stimulus jack the thing up."

"Pavlov's…all the years…hey, wait, you're Vincenzo Longhorn."

"Yeah."

"*You* can't get a dick reduction. That's like Wilt Chamberlain wanting to not be so tall. Or Kobe Bryant not wanting to be quick. You need to live life to the fullest abilities of your talents, like those guys."

"They both died early."

"Yeah, but not because of their gifts."

Vincenzo sipped his coffee a moment and said, "Besides basketball, name one other thing Wilt Chamberlain did of worth."

"He nailed like 40,000 women."

"So have I. That's not anything of worth. It's freakish. That's all I am to people. A giant dick. Nothing more. All I hear is, *Show us your dick.* And, *Can I get a picture with your dick?* Do you know the last time someone was able to look me in the eye for more than five minutes before their eyes linger down to my crotch?"

"So that's why you've been following me?" Petite said.

"Yeah."

"Why didn't you just call my office?"

"I told you, I was embarrassed."

Petite said, "You've been in hundreds of movies with your dick out—"

"Thousands."

"Thousands? Like more than a single thousand?"

"2,112."

"Two thousand? Holy shit...."

"Yeah."

"Anyway, you've been in thousands of movies with your dick out, and you're embarrassed to call a doctor's office about your dick?"

"Apparently."

"Why didn't you just stop by the office and ask to speak to me privately?"

"I didn't know where your office was."

"Why didn't you Google it?"

"Didn't think of that."

"How did you know my home address?"

"Googled it."

"Do you have a hard on right now?" Petite asked in his doctorly voice.

"No, why?"

"Because you said too much blood runs from your brain when you have an erection."

"And?"

"Well what you just said was kind of…nothing. I was just pointing out a fact."

"See?" Vincenzo said, "It's always about my dick."

"Well, we were just talking about your dick," Petite said defensively. As he watched the flatbed pull away with his Tesla, he shifted gears back to his doctor voice, "Look, I will leave your name with my secretary. Call the office and make an appointment; you don't have to tell them what it's for."

"Really?"

"Yes."

"Thanks, man."

A sedan pulled up to the adjacent curb, the driver looking at his phone as if for confirmation.

"Looks like my Uber is here," Petite said. "You need a lift somewhere?"

"Nah. The firemen were nice enough to put a charge in my car. Good guys. Didn't cost me much for them to do it."

"They charged you money?"

"No. I just had to pose with them, while holding the fire hose like a dick."

Petite watched Vincenzo for a moment, then said,

"Call my office."

"Okay."

"I'll be seeing you, Vincenzo."

"Not if I see you first, Dr. Petite."

"That sounds a little like you're going to follow me again," Petite said.

"Nah, I'm done with that," Vincenzo said.

Chapter 15

She'd called him, saying they needed to meet, and now he sat in his IROC, parked down the street from the Petite's home. He was turning up the volume on "She's Like the Wind" when Vivian jumped into the passenger seat like a sudden hurricane, fury and beauty combined.

Vincenzo jerked. "Jesus."

"Drive," she said.

"Where?"

"I don't know. Drive in circles. Pretend you're tailing my husband."

Vincenzo shifted into first and drove down the road. "You sound mad," he said.

"You think?"

"You sound really mad."

"I am really mad, Vincenzo. You get into a car chase with my husband and blow up his Tesla?"

"I didn't blow up his Tesla. Thing just burst into flames."

"And then you tell him—a man with a micro-penis —that you have a fourteen inch cock?"

"We were bonding. He turned out to be a pretty good guy. I think he really got me."

"Really? He got you? He said you didn't have enough blood in your body to run your dick and brain at the same time."

"Isn't that like information falling under confidentiality or something?"

"Then he said it wouldn't matter, even without the giant dick, you'd be the dumbest person in the world."

"Really? He said that?"

"He said you were the Wilt Chamberlain of idiots; whatever that means."

"I guess it means I'm the GOAT of idiots? Or maybe that I've like fucked 40,000 idiots?"

"And the cost of your little stunt is me getting another procedure. And the sex with him is getting rougher. One might even call it rape."

"He raped you? Can a husband rape his wife?"

"Of course a husband can rape his wife."

"I don't know. I'm not a rape expert; I don't fucking rape people."

"Well if someone doesn't want to have sex and you force them to have sex, then it's rape."

"That, like, happened to me all the time. Never mattered if my dick was hurting or chaffed or whatever, it's always, *Vincenzo get in there and fuck that pussy.* They even once splinted my dick erect when—" He glanced from the road to her. She was glaring at him. He said, "Never mind."

"Do you want me?" Vivian said.

"Of course I do."

"Do you want to be with me?"

"More than anything."

"Well there isn't going to be much of me left to be with soon." She broke into tears, covering her face.

"Hey, hey," Vincenzo said. Steering the car with one hand, he rubbed her back with the other. "It's going to be okay. I can get the gun. We can do this. I'll figure it out."

She continued to sob into her hands. "I just want us to be the way we were on that first day. Quipping back and forth without a care for the past or the future. Just the present of you and me."

"Yeah. Yeah. We can have that."

"Promise?" she sobbed.

"I promise."

She looked up from her hands and forced a smile through her tears.

"Okay?" Vincenzo said.

"Okay," she said. She glanced around and said, "Why are we in a dead end alleyway?"

"You said to pretend I was following your husband. This is where we ended up. Hey, there's a place with great egg sandwiches around the corner from here. You want one?"

Chapter 16

Kraken handed Vincenzo the .44 Magnum. "Here," he said. "Go off and hunt grouse or whatever it is you want this thing for."

"You know what I want it for."

"No. No I don't."

"I want it to kill Vivian Petite's husband, who lives at 496 Harrison Blvd., phone number—"

"Jesus, stop. I don't want to be remotely involved in any of this."

When Vincenzo caught a glimpse of his image in the mirror over Kraken's couch, he pointed the gun and said, "You talking to me? I don't see anyone else here, you talki—"

"Do you even know how to use that thing?"

"Yeah. You point it and pull the trigger."

"Fucking amateur. You don't go waving and pointing a gun around. I have neighbors next door and you're pointing a .44 Magnum at the wall playing like you're Travis Bickle."

"Who's Travis Bickle?"

"*Taxi Driver*?"

"You have a taxi driver named Travis Bickle?"

"The movie; you were just doing the thing."

"What thing?"

"The Taxi Driver thi—never mind, just stop pointing the gun around."

"Is it loaded?" Vincenzo said, turning the gun's barrel toward his face and inspecting the revolver's chambers.

"Fuck, man," Kraken said, snatching the gun out of Vincenzo's hand.

"What? I can see there's no bullets in the holes there."

"No such thing as an unloaded gun. Jesus, you're gonna end up shooting your dick off with this thing aren't you?"

"No. I'm going to shoot Herman Peti—"

"Stop," Kraken squeaked. "Please, just stop."

"Do you have the bullets?"

"Yes," Kraken said, tossing the rounds onto the couch, the bullets dancing and jiggling inside their box.

Vincenzo held his hand out, staring at his friend, and Kraken reluctantly handed the gun back to him.

Vincenzo struggled with opening the cylinder, smacking it with his palm. "How does this thing open?"

"You're like a fucking ape." Kraken snatched the Magnum back and thumbed the cylinder release. It fell open. "See?"

"Cool," Vincenzo said, snatching the box of rounds from the couch.

Kraken snapped the cylinder shut again. "Nope. You can load it well outside of my apartment. In fact, I'd prefer if you did it well outside the city limits."

"Fine," Vincenzo said, snatching the gun back.

"I thought you told me you'd used a gun before."

"I did. It was a prop gun. Someone else loaded the thing. I just pointed it and pulled the trigger."

Kraken shook his head. "I know you're gonna shoot your dick off with that thing."

Chapter 17

Vincenzo didn't exactly "shoot his dick off" in that dark bar with Vivian sitting beside him. It was more a graze of its shaft, and he forked his ballsack—luckily leaving the testicles intact.

While lying in his hospital room with a bag of ice on his crotch, the nurse told him someone was here to see him.

Vincenzo said, "More cops? I already told them it was an accident, and I didn't know the girl I was in the bar with."

The nurse said, "No. It's a woman here to see you."

"Is it Vivian Petite, the girl from the bar...? Whom I don't know."

"I don't know who she is," the nurse said.

"Neither do I," Vincenzo said with a wink.

"Okay," the nurse said. "Then I'll let her in."

Vincenzo shifted, painfully, and smoothed his hair. He snatched up the polished metal of the bedpan and inspected his appearance.

But it wasn't Vivian who came into the room.

"Gina," Vincenzo said to his former castmate.

Gina glanced at the bedpan in his hand and said, "Should I come back?"

"Oh, no," Vincenzo said and set the bedpan aside.

"I didn't think they still used metal bedpans," Gina said.

"Nothing but the best for me, I guess," Vincenzo said with a shrug. He then said, "So what brings you here, Gina?"

"You, dummy."

"Me?"

"Yeah. I heard the great Vincenzo Longhorn shot his dick off. Thought I'd pay my respects."

"Nah, just grazed it," Vincenzo said. "But how did you hear about it?"

"When you're part of a tribe, word travels fast."

"Tribe?"

"Adult performers."

"Who else knows?"

"Everyone knows. There's a candlelight vigil tonight."

"But I'm not dead."

"It's the dick everyone is concerned about."

"Gee, thanks. Shit, is this going to kill my career?"

"It only sets the stage for a triumphant return."

"Damn. I don't know if I'm ready for that." Vincenzo hung his head.

"Vincenzo," Gina said, "I'm fucking with you. I found out because I'm dating a cop. He told me."

"You're dating a cop?"

"Uh-huh."

"Is he good to you?"

"Nope," Gina said. "And if I were to guess, I'd say you shot your dick over some woman who isn't good for you."

"She's perfect for me," Vincenzo said.

"Perfect for you doesn't mean good for you."

"Suppose not."

"So catch me up," Gina said, sitting on the side of his bed.

Vincenzo groaned as his body shifted with her weight on the bed. "Jesus," he said. "Do you mind?"

"Aw, am I causing a little pain in your nether-regions? Now you know what it's like getting rammed by a fourteen-inch dick. Toughen up."

"This is different," Vincenzo said.

"Not that different."

"It hurt that bad? Fucking me, I mean?"

"Um, yeah," Gina said as if it were the most obvious of facts.

"But you acted like you enjoyed it."

"What's the key word in that sentence?"

"*You?*"

"Try again."

"*Enjoyed?*"

"One more time."

Vincenzo looked to the ceiling, recalling the sentence, and counted on his fingers as he mouthed the words. "*It?*" he said.

"*Acted,* shithead. I was *acting.*"

"Wow. You're a pretty good actress then."

"Most women are."

"Really?"

"Yes."

"Huh," Vincenzo said, as if learning an obscure historical fact.

"Tell me about this woman you shot your dick off for. Allegedly."

"Allegedly? I'm in the hospital aren't I?"

"Yeah. I don't doubt the shooting part, but come on, she shot you, right? What did you do?"

"Nothing. She didn't shoot me."

"Jealous husband?"

"No."

"C'mon, no one is dumb enough to shoot themselves in their own dick." Gina guffawed with a lilting harmonic laugh, accentuated with a few snorts.

Her laughter faded when Vincenzo hung his head.

"Oh…" Gina said. "Okay. I guess accidents can happen, I mean…so what did happen?"

"I was just showing off my gun. And it went off."

"If I were talking to you at any other time, I would take that as innuendo, double entendre, what have you."

Vincenzo scoffed. "Like that gun ever went off accidentally."

"Why do you have a gun?"

"Huh?"

"Why do you have a gun…? The real gun. Why do you have it?"

"Long story."

"Meaning it's a short story, but you don't want to tell it."

"Something like that."

"Well, if I may, I think you are the last person who should have a gun."

"Why's that?"

"I saw you on the set of *Dick Me, My Darling*, remember? You were waving that thing around like you were Yosemite Sam."

"What, my dick?"

"No. The gun…and your dick."

"I was practicing my quick-draw. And getting pretty good at it, I might add."

"Yeah, if you were quick-drawing to shoot off your own di—wait, is that what happened? Did you quick-draw your dick off?"

"I didn't shoot my dick off. And, no. I was hiding the gun under the table and it accidentally went off."

"Oh brother. Gun safety 101."

"How do you know so much about this?"

"Because my father was a drunk who loved whiskey and guns. And he might have taught me a thing or two. Especially that quick-draws usually end up with a bullet in your foot. Or, I suppose for you, your dick."

"A porn star with a gun-toting alcoholic father, how original," Vincenzo muttered.

"He was also a fucking saint, asshole. Are you going to insult me, or let me talk?"

"Sorry," Vincenzo said. "That was out of line."

"I know you only get out of line when your ego is hurt, so apology accepted," Gina said, leaning over and pinching Vincenzo's cheek. She then slapped him gently on the cheek, saying, "But do it again, and I will punch you in your tender dick right now."

"Noted," Vincenzo groaned. "You were saying?"

"I was saying, the key to firing a gun is remembering that slow and steady breathing makes a slow and steady hand. Wyatt Earp couldn't quick draw shit. You ever see that fucker's gun? He wouldn't even be able to clear his holster in time. But that didn't matter. He stayed calm. While everyone else rushed to shoot him, they sprayed bullets everywhere, but he breathed slow and steady and aimed for a kill every fucking time. You panicked to hide the gun—for some reason I probably don't want to know about—and you shot your dick off. Next time breathe slow and steady. Or don't be in a situation where you need to suddenly flail a gun around like an idiot."

"Yeah, well, I probably won't be needing to show my gun off any time soon anyway. I'm sure the girl is out on me. I keep fucking up. I mean, with the putting those old ladies in the hospital, the car chases, blowing up her husband's car, shooting my dick…I'm not sure she wants anything to do with me anym—" He stopped when he spotted Gina's gaping expression. "What?" he said.

"That's, um, a lot," Gina said. "How long have you known this woman?"

"A week."

"What?" Gina stood suddenly from the bed, causing Vincenzo to shift and groan. She chortled and said, "Jesus, a Vincenzo special."

"What does that mean?"

"You pick the doozies. Hey, I know I'm throwing stones from a glass house here, but…" She chortled again. "Wow."

"I love her. And she loves me." He looked down, dejected. "At least she did. She was going to leave her husband for me."

"What's her husband do?"

"He's some super rich plastic surgeon with a tiny penis."

"Aw, sweetie, sounds like she just wanted some wild sex. She's having some fun and then she'll—"

"No. There is no sex. She can't. Her pussy is too tight."

Gina looked at him like a parent explaining the truth about Santa Claus. "Hon," she said, rubbing his leg, "I think you might be her rape fantasy."

"No. She doesn't like rape. She told me."

"No woman likes rape, you fucking idiot." She sat down in the chair beside the bed. "But many, maybe even most, women have a rape fantasy of some kind. At least, straight women do."

"But I thought rape was bad."

"It is fucking bad, you moron. What's the matter with you?"

"Why are you yelling at me?"

"Because you're being an idiot man right now."

"Well, I'm confused. I mean, I've never heard of a rape fantasy. I don't have them, okay?"

"If you had a rape fantasy, you'd be a sick fuck."

"But you have them?"

"No, asshole. I've actually been raped. Get your head out of your ass."

Vincenzo put his head in his hands and groaned. "You've somehow made my head hurt worse than my dick right now."

"Look, most straight suburban women have some kind of fantasy where a brute takes them by force. The key is, the women actually want him, so it's not creepy rape, it's just good hard sex with a stranger, usually a stranger with a big dick. Rape fantasy is an unfortunate term, I know. Think of it more as the Fabio-syndrome. You know, big dude ripping off your clothes on a moonlit beach or something."

"I had no idea."

"Well, if we made movies whose target audience were women instead of men, then that's what you would have been doing in them all these years."

"Being Fabio?"

"Yes, probably. Point is, you are her Fabio, and she will leave you when it gets too real."

"Really?"

"Yes."

"And that's a Vincenzo Special?"

"Not that specifically. A Vincenzo Special is just the worst possible woman for Vincenzo. Which is pretty much every woman you are attracted to."

"What do I do? Give up women?"

"Fuck no. Men are worse."

"Do you have a Gina Special?"

"Of course I do. Dating one now. Controlling, abusive, domineering, thinks he has a big dick…a lot of people in our industry have a special."

"Why is that?"

"I think we fuck so much, and play the parts so much, we've lost our sense of…I don't know, we've lost sight of intimacy…the quiet real connections. We're like junkies looking to find meaning in the high, and we keep chasing a higher high. And we latch onto things in people that might not be real. I don't know." She shrugged.

"So there are a lot of us with Vincenzo Specials?"

"God, no. You take it to another level. Your specials are…special."

"Why?"

"Well, *you're* kind of…special." Gina squinched up her face when saying this word.

"Special? Like special needs, special?"

"No. Naïve is more like it."

"You think I'm dumb?"

"No. No, Vincenzo; you're not dumb. You're

just…simple."

Vincenzo winced.

"No, no, no. Not like that," Gina said. "You just view things in the simplest ways. It's a good thing. You're just…trusting that things around you are really the way you think they are."

"So…dumb."

"No. Look, we adult performers basically spend our twenties and thirties in a world where pizza delivery guys accidentally stumble into lesbian pillow fights."

"Hey, like *Lesbo Pillow Fight Four-way Four-play*."

"Yes, Vincenzo, just like *Lesbo Pillow Fight Four-way Four-play*. The point is, you kind of act like the pizza guy from *Lesbo Pillow Fight Four-way Four-play* in real life."

"I've never delivered pizza."

Gina watched her friend a moment and then stood. She stepped over to the bed and kissed Vincenzo on the forehead. "Just be careful, buddy," she said. She turned and walked toward the door.

"I'm never careful…" Vincenzo began, and Gina, about to exit the room, turned to finish their catch phrase, "Careful is boring."

She blew him a kiss and left the room.

Chapter 18

Vincenzo had been home for three days, ice pack clasped to his balls. During that time, he hadn't received a single call from Vivian. On the third day, he finally began to feel like himself again. And late that night, he received a call from what the caller ID said was Herman Petite.

"Hello?" He said in the manner of checking if someone is asleep.

"*Vincenzo?*" It was Vivian's voice.

"Hey, nice of you to call. Why didn't—?"

"*Vincenzo,*" she said again.

"Why are you whispering? And out of breath?"

"*I need help.*"

"With what?"

"*I need help,*" she said again.

"You said that. With what?"

"*He's…he's gotten worse. I'm scared.*"

"Scared of what?"

"*He's going to kill me.*"

"He said he was going to kill you?"

"*No. It's in his eyes. He's gotten angrier and angrier since you told him about your fourteen-inch dick. He raped me.*"

"And it wasn't the good kind?"

"*What?*" she squeaked. "*The good kind?*"

"You know, Fabio…?"

"*He's been beating me, Vincenzo.*"

"All right. Are you in danger right now?"

"*Yes. I think so. There's a look in his eyes. I'm hiding now.*"

"Why don't you call the cops?"

"*They all play golf with him. They won't believe me.*"

"Shit." He shifted uncomfortably in his chair. "Then I'll come and get you."

"*Bring your Dirty Harry gun. He's been walking around with his peashooter. I'll leave the back door unlocked and turn the alarm off.*"

"If you can get to the door, then why don't you just sneak out and I can pick you up?"

"*I thought we were going to take care of this together?*"

"Well, yeah…but, you know, it'd be kind of better if it were planned out and all. And I just got a beer, and my ice pack—"

"*Are you serious right now?*"

"Well, yeah. I mean, I did shoot my dick and all."

Her voice suddenly rose in panic as she said, "*Oh no, he's coming this way. Please, Vincenzo. Please end this. I need you. I need your hel—*"

The line went dead.

"Hello?" Vincenzo said.

But she was gone.

Chapter 19

Vincenzo parked down the street from the Petites' house, and he now stood beside the wall surrounding the property. It was about eight feet tall. Easy enough for someone to pop over. At least, easy enough for someone who had not been shot in the nutsack. He supposed he could scale the thing, but swinging his legs over its top? His crotch throbbed just thinking about it.

He slinked beside the wall, searching for vulnerabilities. Maybe he could scale it and catch hold of one of those tree branches that hung over the wall's edge. But still, the thought of hoisting his dangling bodyweight throbbed his nethers again.

Maybe he could get a rope and construct a kind of pulley system?

Or find a long plank and create a ramp?

Maybe the front gate's wrought iron bars would make for a good ladder?

The thought of being impaled on the wrought iron spears sent panic through his being.

Maybe he could find some dynamite?

He stopped. A small door, which was embedded in the side of the wall, had been left open.

He glanced up and down the sidewalk, as if looking for the fairy godmother who'd granted him this access, and he stepped through the door.

Within the wall, he lingered in a small tree line, which edged the property's outer barrier. He could now see the house, dark in the inky blackness of night. A dim light was on toward the back of the dwelling. Perhaps the door she said she'd leave unlocked?

He drew the .44 Magnum from the band of his pants, and darted, bent over—partly due to subterfuge, partly because his nuts ached—toward the light. Halfway to the house, he stopped, noticing the sudden flicker of a red light. A security camera. After peering at it like a spooked owl for a few seconds, he turned around and shuffled the remaining distance to the house backwards.

Reaching the dim light at the back of the house, he peered through the window. It was a light in a large range hood over a large stove in a large kitchen. He shuffled over to the door beside the window. Did she leave it unlocked? And more importantly, did she turn off the security alarm? He glanced over his shoulder for any more flickers of red before realizing that this act would only make his face clearer on any footage. He lowered his head, placed his hand on the doorknob, and pushed.

The door opened.

He paused in the doorway, waiting for the blare of a security alarm.

But there was only silence.

Vivian had successfully disarmed the alarm. Or the alarm was silent. He glanced over his shoulder toward the property's outer wall, and the bustling world outside its border. No sign of trouble—no police sirens, or ravenous guard dogs, or muscle-bound henchmen. He wanted to glance over his other shoulder, but remembering the camera, thought better of it.

Stepping over the threshold, he entered the kitchen, testing his weight on the floor to be sure it didn't creak—a habit he'd learned as a kid when sneaking back into his house after sneaking out at night. He tiptoed his way through the kitchen—sure not to disturb any wayward pot or knock over an unseen glass—a tightrope walker over the abyss.

At the far end of the kitchen, a pair of open French doors led into another room. Vincenzo made his way to them and peered into the next room, which was barely illuminated from the light in the kitchen and the moonlight through the windows. Tightroping through this darker abyss, he made his way to a large open space, barely perceptible in the moonlight.

"Vivian," he whispered.

Silence.

Vincenzo groped his way through the darkness, wishing he had a flashlight, when he remembered he had his cellphone. He held up the phone and pressed the side button and the screen illuminated a swath of darkness, enough for Vincenzo to get around a couch before the light clicked off.

The subsequent darkness brought a man's voice, saying, "Don't move."

Vincenzo didn't move.

"I am armed," the voice said.

"I am too," Vincenzo said.

"I have a gun," the man's voice said.

"I do too," Vincenzo said.

"My gun is bigger," the man said.

"I doubt that," Vincenzo said.

A light filled the room, like an atomic blast to Vincenzo's unaccustomed eyes. When he blinked away the flashing cobwebs, he found Herman Petite holding the biggest handgun Vincenzo had ever seen.

"Vincenzo?" Petite said.

"Jesus Christ, that gun is huge," Vincenzo said. "What the fuck is that thing?"

"Desert Eagle .50."

"It looks like *Robocop's* gun."

"I think they might have used one in *Robocop*."

"Oh, really?"

"What do you have there? Is that a .44 Magnum?" Petite said.

"Yeah. Just like Dirty Harry's."

"Wasn't Dirty Harry's silver?"

"That's what I thought. Turns out it was black."

"You've got to be careful with those double-action

guns. You draw too quick and it's liable to go off by accident."

"You're telling me. I nearly shot my nuts off with this thing."

"No shit? Well, that certainly would have saved you some money on that penis reduction."

The two of them laughed. Then the laughter faded a little awkwardly.

"So…" Herman said. "Why are you in my house with Dirty Harry's gun?"

"Where is she?" Vincenzo said, leveling his gun onto Petite.

"Who?"

"Vivian. What have you done with her?"

"Vivi—fuck, man, are you screwing my wife? Wait, that's not possible, I'd have known."

"So you *are* performing those procedures on her?"

"The fuck? How do you—?" Petite said. He stopped and called over his shoulder, "Vivian? Hey, Vivian, get down here." He then said to Vincenzo, "How the hell do you know Vivian?"

"She came to one of my seminars last week."

"Last week? She didn't go anywhere last week," he said. He called over his shoulder again, "Vivian?"

"Well she did go somewhere last week," Vincenzo said, "And—" He stopped short as a tall woman with doe eyes and long cascading black hair entered the room. There was silence for what seemed a day before Vincenzo said, "No. No. Where's Vivian? Your wife."

"This is Vivian," Petite said. "My wife."

"No. The blonde."

"Blonde?"

"You know, the blonde woman. The beatings? The procedures? Your tiny dick?"

"My tiny dick? You told him about my tiny dick?" Petite said, turning to his wife.

"No, this isn't Vivi—" Vincenzo began, gesturing toward the woman with the barrel of his gun, but he didn't get a chance to finish as he heard a loud crash and what seemed to be a bee buzzing past his ear. There was a woman's scream, and with the second crash, Vincenzo realized Petite was shooting at him. Or at least in his general direction. The bullets sprayed, shattering and exploding objects behind him.

Vincenzo took a deep breath and let it out. He felt immediate calm wash over him, and he raised the .44 Magnum.

He fired.

Petite dropped to the floor.

The woman screamed.

Then silence.

Vincenzo stepped over to the body. A bloody hole bulls-eyed Petite's heart.

"Oh my God," the woman said, covering her mouth.

Vincenzo shifted his gun to point at her. "Who are you? Where's Vivian?"

"I'm Vivian," the woman said, lowering her hands from her face.

"No you're not."

"Yes, I am. I'm Vivian."

"Where is she?" Vincenzo said, his voice rising into a growl.

"I'm Vivian," the woman said. "Don't you recognize me, Vincenzo?" The woman spread her arms in a welcoming manner.

"Huh?" Vincenzo said. "You're not…" He looked down at his feet for a moment. "No, you're—"

"Vivian," the woman said. "Remember? We met a week ago. At your seminar."

"But—"

"Remember our walk along the waterfront? You putting the old ladies in the hospital by exposing your dick? Us in the bar when you nearly shot your dick off?"

"No…no, that's not…that wasn't you."

"It *was* me."

"No," Vincenzo said. He felt dizzy, like his legs were about to give out. He was the lone sailor on a sinking boat in angry tempest seas. What was happening?

"Why don't you recognize me, Vincenzo?"

"I…I don't know." He put his hand to his head, smacking his skull with the .44 Magnum.

Vivian took the gun out of his hand. "Careful with that."

He looked at his hands, focusing on them, something real.

"Are you okay, Vincenzo?" Vivian said.

"No," he said. "Is this like a Vanilla Sky kind of thing,

or am I going crazy?"

"You were right," the dark-haired Vivian said. "He is kinda simple."

"Huh?" Vincenzo said.

"I said dumb," a voice came from behind Vincenzo.

Vincenzo spun around and saw Vivian—*his* Vivian—standing over Petite's corpse. She held the Desert Eagle hip-high, pointed at Vincenzo. She said, "Alexa, play jazz." Jazz began playing from a sound system. "For old times' sake," she said.

"Vivian," Vincenzo said. "What—?"

"She wasn't lying," the blonde woman said to Vincenzo, nodding at the woman with the long dark hair. "*She* is Vivian."

Vincenzo said, "Alexa, play *Chinatown*."

The theme of *Chinatown* came over the sound system.

The blonde woman nodded with a mischievous mouth shrug, and said, "Touché."

"Then who are you?" Vincenzo said.

"I'm Beate Lindgren," the blond said. "I'd shake your hand in introduction, but I have this giant gun in it and all."

Vincenzo looked at his hand, barely remembering handing his own gun over to Vivian. The *real* Vivian.

"But why…? Wait…Beat Lindgren…?" Vincenzo said.

"It's Beate, like be-ought-a"

"Where have I heard that name?"

"Probably *Sports Illustrated*," Beate said.

"Swimsuit model?" Vincenzo said.

"Tennis star," Beate said. "And swimsuit model."

"Oh, yeah. I remember you. I Beate off to your picture quite a bit."

"Did you just come up with that?"

"Nah. I think I heard that one a while back. But you were, like, really hot."

"*I was* really hot?" Beate said.

"Well, obviously you still are. I mean, I just shot a guy over you. But, yeah…I definitely remember that swimsuit issue."

"Yeah, that damn swimsuit issue. People forget I also played tennis," she said. "I was quite good, too. Even beat Monica Seles. But I tended to be compared more with Anna Kournikova than Steffi Graf. And once the Williams Sisters came along to kick everyone's ass, and a younger Sharapova began gracing the magazine covers, I was all but forgotten. Now I've been relegated to teaching old ladies to swing futilely at tennis balls at a country club."

"So you *worked* there?"

"Yup. A lowly servant. But it wasn't all bad; I did get to meet some great people." She glanced over at Vivian, and the two shared a look that Vincenzo immediately recognized.

"Oh, so you two…" he pointed his finger back and forth as if keeping track of which factors to multiply in a complicated math problem. "So all this was a setup? You tricked me into shooting a man I had no ire against so you two can run off with his money?"

"Did you say no ire?" Beate said.

"Yes. Why?"

"Just a strange use of words."

"So you made up the abuse and the rape just to trick me?"

"No," Vivian, the real Vivian, said. "He did abuse me. He did rape me. The procedures, all of it was real."

"And the micro penis?"

"Real."

"Thank God. Would have been disappointing if that part was fake. Was it, like, really micro?"

Vivian nodded.

"Like seriously? Like, what, index finger?"

"Tip of the pinky," Vivian said.

"Wow. Poor guy."

"Poor guy?" Beate said. "She was abused because that *poor guy* couldn't handle his dick size. And now you know why we chose *you* to be the patsy."

"Huh? Me?"

"Yes, you, Mr. *Longhorn*," Beate said. "Who do you think made him so insecure about his tiny penis?"

Vincenzo gave the question a moment's consideration and shrugged. "I don't know, his parents? God?"

"*You*," Beate practically shouted.

"Me? How did I make his dick small?"

"You didn't make his dick small. You helped make *him* small. You and all those dudes like you waving your giant dicks around like you're Fred Astaire with a fucking cane. I'd only known you for one day and I'd already seen your dick like four times."

"I think it was more like two times…maybe three at the most."

"I'm a lesbian; I shouldn't have to see a dick at all."

"Well, I mean, you did come to a *sex* seminar with a guy named Vincenzo *Longhorn.* I wouldn't come to a tennis lesson and not expect to see your racquet."

"The point is, for you, your manhood is a tool. A weapon. And it made *him*," she pointed at the corpse on the floor, "violent, vindictive, and vile."

"Maybe he was all those things because he was just an asshole. It seems kind of like a chicken and egg thing."

"Look, you can't live a life having your dick represent the entirety of male aggression, and then say it wasn't your fault in the end."

"The end? So you're going to kill me?"

"Sorry, Vince, you really are a pretty decent guy and all—aside from just murdering her husband—" she nodded toward Vivian, "but the plan doesn't work unless you're dead."

"What plan? Do I at least get to hear the plan? Because I gotta be honest, it doesn't really sound like that solid of a plan."

"Pretty simple plan, actually" Beate said. "We're going to make it look like you and Herman were in cahoots to murder Vivian."

"Murder Vivian? How do you intend to do that?"

"Well, we've been establishing a connection between the two of you for some time now. The phone number I've been calling you from and the one you've been calling are to and from *his* phones." She nodded toward the corpse.

"How did he not notice that?"

"We just erased the number. It's not like he ever looked at the bill. But the cops will look, and see your number, making it look like you two knew each other. There has also been money wired from his account to a dummy account, making it look like you two had some kind of deal going. A deal to kill his wife." She nodded toward Vivian. "And with the abuse she's been subjected to, that will be easy enough to prove."

"Okay…so…I don't get it."

Beate said, "So, the two of you had a deal going, and something went wrong."

"What went wrong?"

"It doesn't matter."

"It kind of matters."

"No. It doesn't matter because you'll both be dead. It could be anything. Maybe you were gay lovers."

"You're gonna let me go down with the humiliation of being that guy's gay lover?"

"You have a problem with gay lovers? You find that humiliating?"

"Nah, it's not the gay part. It's the rich asshole with a tiny dick part that's humiliating. I couldn't do better than him?"

"Fine. Maybe you weren't lovers. Maybe…I don't know, the deal went sour or something."

"Yeah, that sounds better," Vincenzo said.

"It turns out," Beate said, "your dumb move of getting into a car chase with him only solidified our plan. You and he were now witnessed together by the police and fire department. There really are no loose ends."

"What about all the people who saw you and me together?" Vincenzo said. "The waitress…the other waitress…the old ladies, everyone at the seminar, everyone at your club?"

"I'll tell them that you must have been trying to use me to get closer to *her*." She nodded toward Vivian. "I mean, you did sneak into the club wearing a valet jacket. Again, I can say whatever I want because you'll be dead."

"Well…yeah, I guess that is a pretty solid plan," Vincenzo said.

"I like to think so," Beate said, sounding quite proud of herself. "So if you don't mind, I actually need you to move back over where you were when you shot Herman."

"Huh? Why?"

"So the forensics line up and it looks like you shot each other."

"Oh, yeah, that makes sense," Vincenzo said. He walked toward the spot where he'd been standing. "What if he *had* shot me?" he asked.

"Then I would have come in and shot Herman with your gun."

"Yeah," Vincenzo said, nodding. "I guess that works too." He looked at Vivian and said, "You don't talk much, do you?"

"Me?" Vivian said.

"Yeah. Seems like she's doing all the talking," he said, gesturing toward Beate.

Vivian shrugged and said, "I guess so."

"She says *I* a lot too. *I* did this. *I* did that," Vincenzo said.

"So what?" Beate said with a growl of defensiveness.

Vincenzo shrugged. "Just seems like it's *your* plan," he said to Beate.

"So what if it is?" Beate said.

"Her money," he said, gesturing toward Vivian, "and your plan?" He gestured toward Beate.

"It's called teamwork," Beate said.

"You seem more like a coach than a teammate," Vincenzo said.

"Yes, I am like a coach," Beate said. "I'm helping her along."

"No, I don't mean like a tennis coach," Vincenzo said. "I mean like a football coach, where you're calling all the plays."

"What? No, that's not what it…will you…look, move over a little," Beate said, waving her hand.

"Huh?"

"You were standing a little more that way," she said, pointing.

"It was here," he said.

"No, it was further that way," Beate said. "C'mon, this has to line up perfectly for the forensics."

"I'm pretty sure it was here," he said.

"Pretty sure isn't good enough," Beate said. "It has to be exact for this to work."

"I'm telling you, I was standing right here," Vincenzo said. With his finger, he mimicked drawing a gun up to shoot.

"No. It was that way," Beate said.

"I think he's right," Vivian said.

"What's that?" Beate snapped.

"I think that's where he was," Vivian said in a quiet voice.

"Well *I* think he was over a little," Beate said.

"But you weren't here," Vivian said. "We were." She fluttered her index finger between herself and Vincenzo.

"Whose side are you on?" Beate said.

"Obviously your side. *You* want to get it right, right?"

"He's trying to trick us by saying he was where he wasn't."

"I don't think he *is* trying to trick us."

"I'm actually not," Vincenzo said. "Although that probably would have been a good idea."

"See?" Vivian said.

"Fine, take the *man's* side," Beate said.

"I'm not taking any side," Vivian said.

Beate groaned and said, "Whatever." She turned to Vincenzo and held the gun up in a standard thumbs-forward grip.

"Huh," Vincenzo mused with a chuckle. "All that time I spent trying to fuck you, and it turns out you fucked me."

"Sorry, Vincenzo."

"Can I just say one more thing?" Vincenzo said.

Beate sighed and said, "Fine. What is it?"

"It's to you," he said to Vivian.

"Me?"

"Yeah."

"What is it?"

"Just a word of advice."

"Okay."

"If I learned anything in my industry, it's that fuckers are gonna fuck."

"I'm not sure I know what that means."

"I have a feeling you will," Vincenzo said.

"Goodbye, Vincenzo," Beate said.

Vincenzo said, "Oh, you forgot about—" But before he could finish Beate pulled the trigger, the roar of the gun drowning out Vivian's scream.

Vincenzo dropped to the floor, dead.

"Oh my God," Vivian said, covering her mouth. "You did it."

"I had to," Beate said.

"I know, but…oh my God."

"It's done. We have to keep moving forward," Beate said.

"Oh my God," Vivian said again, covering her mouth.

"Hey," Beate said gently, gripping Vivian's shoulder. "Don't worry. We just committed the perfect murder. There are no loose ends. It's just you and me now."

"But it sounded like he was going to say something else."

"Yeah, some bullshit," Beate said.

"Sounded like he was going to tell us something important."

"Believe me, that is the last guy that had something important to say."

"He said we forgot something. Are you sure there's no loose ends?" Vivian said.

"Positive."

Chapter 20

The headline read:

PROMINENT DOCTOR AND FORMER PORN STAR KILL EACH OTHER IN BOTCHED PLOT TO MURDER DOCTOR'S WIFE.

The article outlined how noted plastic surgeon Herman Petite had contracted former porn star Vincenzo Longhorn to murder Petite's wife Vivian (photo provided), but the men shot one another when the deal went sour. Vivian, who is set to inherit the doctor's fortune after years of abuse, says she'd never even heard of the former adult star, and she plans to leave the public eye, moving to Costa Rica, as soon as her husband's affairs are taken care of.

After finishing the article, Kraken leaned back in his chair, muttering, "Never heard of him, huh?" He glanced at the bag of firearms he had on the kitchen table—his new business venture—and sighed, saying, "I knew I was going to get dragged into this somehow."

Available Now

Pacifier Politics: Chronicle of a Baby President

Find it now on **stonepulp.com**
Read Episode One Here:

Marybeth Fredrickson opened the front door. Two men stood on the other side of the screen.

"If you two are like Mormons or something, I'm all set," Marybeth said.

The younger of the two men looked down, inspecting his attire: a store-bought, ill-fitting brown suit. The older of the two, wearing an impeccably tailored blue Brioni, flashed a grin, saying, "Are you Marybeth Fredrickson?"

"I am."

"Your mother was Irene Fredrickson?"

Marybeth paused a moment, biting her lip. "She was," she said.

"I'm very sorry for your loss," the Brioni suit said.

"Very sorry," the brown suit muttered in unison with his partner's sentiment.

"Okay," Marybeth said. "Thank you?"

"We'd like to have a word with you about some loose ends in your mother's affairs. May we come in?"

"And who are you exactly?"

"Oh, I'm sorry. Of course. How rude of me. I am Slick Ives, and this is Irving Sinclair."

"Actually, it's Ernest," the younger man said.

"We are with the P.P.F.L.A.P," Ives said.

"The PP…what?"

"F.L.A.P.," Ives said.

"PP-flap?"

"Ha. No. The P.P.F.L.A.P. Or, I suppose you *could* call it PP-flap if you so wish," Ives added with his bright, toothy grin. "Should we start calling it PP-flap, Irv?"

"Nest…Er-nest," Ernest said. "And probably not."

Ives raised his eyebrows.

Ernest said, "But, sure, you *could* call it PP-flap."

"Perfect," Ives grinned. "PP-flap it is."

"Are you, like, with the government or something?" Marybeth said.

"Not quite," Ives said. "In fact, we are what you might call a government watchdog group. Kind of. Essentially, we watch the government and try to influence them to align more with the people's wishes. In fact, the first P in PP-flap is for *People*."

"What do the other letters stand for?" Marybeth said.

While Ives said, "That's not important right now," Ernest recited, "People's Patriotic Freedoms League for American Patriots."

"What was that?" Marybeth said.

"Again, that's not important," Ives said. "At the moment, anyway. We, of course, can get to that later."

"Is your name really Slick?" Marybeth said.

Ives smiled again, saying, "That it is. It turns out you and I both had mothers who maybe walked the edges of alternative culture. My mother named me after her favorite singer. Had I been a girl, I at least would have had the more mainstream name of Grace."

Both Ives and Marybeth chuckled. Ernest, who had been watching people walking along Marybeth's street, snapped his head back to the conversation. He then looked up as if trying to calculate a bill in his head.

Ives said, "It seems my mother fell victim to the counterculture drug scene of San Francisco. Yours…" he left the statement unfinished.

"What?" Marybeth said.

"We really should discuss this inside," Ives said.

Marybeth opened the front screen and let the men inside. "Please sit down," she said, gesturing to the couch. "Can I get you anything?"

"Oh, no thank you," Ives said, sitting down on the couch.

"I could use a coff—" Ernest said, but stopped as he and his partner regarded each other. "I'm all set," Ernest said, sitting beside Ives.

Marybeth sat in a chair perpendicular to the couch, causing the men, sitting upright with hands on knees, to turn their heads in unison toward her like chicks for a feeding.

"My mother was too young to be part of the counter-culture scene in San Francisco," Marybeth said.

Ives grinned, "True," he said, his hands sliding to hang between his knees as he eased into a position more comfortable. "But there are other things that run counter to our culture. In fact, you could say we have been fighting a battle to save our culture since that first gunshot in Lexington."

"Was there a mass shooting in Kentucky today?" Marybeth said.

"No. Lexington and Concord?"

"New Hampshire?"

Ives grinned. "Ha, no. Massachusetts. The shot heard round the world. The beginning of the fight for our fine culture."

"Oh, yes. Of course. I forgot, sorry," Marybeth said.

"Well, it's understandable," Ives said. "You're from a time when school systems weren't required to teach such victories of American patriotism."

"So, what exactly is it about?" Marybeth said.

"Lexington and Concord?" Ives said.

"No. Why are you here in my living room? Something about my mother?"

Ives flashed his grin. "Oh, of course. I apologize. Yes. Again, my condolences."

"Sorry for your loss," Ernest said, the words synchronized with Ives's condolence.

"Thank you."

"May I ask," Ives said, "did your mother have the

same cancer as your father?"

"My father? How do you…what is this about?"

"Would that matter?" Ernest asked Ives suddenly, as if breaking from deep thought. "You know, for our…purpose…?" His voice trailed off as Ives stared at him again.

"Purpose?" Marybeth said. "What is going on here?"

"I'm sorry," Ives said. "It seems my friend, here, has jumped the gun a little. You'll have to excuse him; he's new to this. The question about your father was benign enough. It was a simple inquiry of genetic disposition to illnesses."

"Genetic disp…what is this? Seriously, what is going on?"

Ives put his hands out, saying, "Again, sorry, I can understand your confusion. I would have liked to have eased a little better into this." He glanced at Ernest, who looked at his hands folded in his lap. Ives said, "Ms. Fredrickson, are you aware of your brother?"

"Brother?"

"Or sister," Ernest said. "At this point we don't know. But hopefully brother."

"What?" Marybeth said.

Ives said, "Look, you were very young when your father died; there are things that aren't always discussed with a child."

Ernest said, "My parents told me my dog Biffy ran away, when really—"

Ives bent his head and scratched his forehead,

while staring at his partner.

"Never mind," Ernest said.

"The point is," Ives said, his smile returning in a sudden fireworks display, "when your father became sick, your parents thought—perhaps a little naively in retrospect—that their union in another child would be the best legacy for your father. So they took the scientific route, creating a viable embryo and freezing it, should the day ever come where your mother wanted another child. Turns out, that day never came."

"How do you—? Did you know my parents?"

"Oh, God no, of course not."

"Then how do you know all of this?"

"Well, there are files and paperwork on this type of thing…and actually, believe it or not, the doctor who performed the procedure is still practicing."

"The doctor? Files? Aren't there laws against accessing people's medical information?"

"Oh, yes, definitely," Ernest said. "I once tried to get information—"

With another stern look from Ives, Ernest stopped.

Ives then said to Marybeth, "As Irving said—"

"Ernest."

"—the answer is yes, under HIPAA, a person's medical information is to be kept private. But with the ratification of the 31st Amendment, there are now a few exceptions, this being one of them."

"The 31st…?"

"You're not familiar with the 31st Amendment?"

"Well, there's been so many of them lately," Mary-beth said. "I've—"

"It's The Personhood Act," Ernest said.

"Oh," Marybeth said.

"So you *have* heard of it?" Ives said.

"Of course I have."

Ives said, "Under the Personhood Act, all frozen embryos are now considered viable U.S. citizens, and are required to be designated a guardian."

"You want me to be declared guardian of my parents' unborn embryo? What does that mean?"

"Well for most people it would require bringing the embryo to term."

"What? You're going to force me to give birth to my brother?"

"Or sister," Ernest said. "But hopefully brother."

Ives said. "We prefer the term *required* rather than *forced*, and it doesn't have to be you; it could be a surrogate, but we'd rather it be you for a higher likelihood of the embryo attaching; I mean, you do have the same genetic makeup as your mother so…."

"This is insane."

"No, technically it is the law, but you are in an incredible amount of luck—given the uniqueness of this situation—because we are willing to pay you a very substantial amount for the pregnancy. Should you give birth that is."

"You're buying IVF babies?"

"Just yours," Ernest said.

"Whoa, hold on a minute," Ives said. "We are not *buying* any babies because that would be highly illegal. You would still be the technical parent of the child. We would just be the caregivers."

"Technically more its staff," Ernest said.

"What? Staff?"

"Irv—"

"Ernest."

"—here, is again getting a little ahead of himself. But I suppose we would technically be your baby's staff."

"This makes—"

Ives said, "Look, Ms. Fredrickson, we intend for your son—"

"Brother," Ernest said. "Or sister. But hopefully brother."

"—to be the next president of the United States."

"You want to groom my brother—"

"Or sister."

"—to be president?"

"Please, there will be no grooming," Ives said. "We are strictly avoiding that term."

"But how will you be its staff? You'll be old, or dead, by the time he—"

"Or she."

"—is old enough…wait, what do you mean *next* president?"

"Turns out, babies poll incredibly high," Ernest said.

"For president?" Marybeth said.

"Well, for anything," Ernest said.

"You want my baby—"

"Your sibling," Ernest said.

"—to be president? As a baby? How can—isn't there an age requirement?"

"Well that's where the uniqueness of your situation comes in," Ives said. "You see, given that the 31st Amendment bestows personhood at the moment of conception, and said conception happened so long ago in your parents' case, technically your brother—"

"Or sister. But hopefully brother."

"—is 35 years old, which is the required age for the presidency."

"You're saying my unborn brother—or sister—is old enough to vote?"

"And drink, and rent a car, and…" Ernest said, but then ducked his head after another look from Ives.

"But how can a baby run the country?"

Ives said, "Well, I mean, come on, the president is more of a figurehead, really. We've had plenty of presidents with absolutely no concept of what is going on. We've had some who nap all day, watch television…."

"Throw up on themselves," Ernest added.

"The key is, your brother…or sister, but hopefully brother, will—"

"Why do you keep saying 'hopefully brother?'"

"A female candidate doesn't poll well," Ernest said.

Ives said, "The key is, your sibling will be the president of the United States, and that can be very beneficial to many, *many* people, especially its mother."

"Sister," Ernest said.

"I don't think I can do this," Marybeth said.

"Can't or won't?" Ives said. "Because if it's *won't*, well, we can technically—legally—make you. But if it's *can't*, that means perhaps there's some negotiating to be done?"

"Is it an ethical problem for you?" Ernest said.

"No," Marybeth said. "It's just an incredibly stupid idea."

"Stupid we can work with," Ives said. "Some of the stupidest ideas have worked out great. Like *8 figures* great."

"Are you saying I could be looking at being paid 8 figures for this?" Marybeth said.

"At minimum," Ives said.

"I think stupid can work," Marybeth said. "When do we start?"

"Well sooner than later, if we're to make the Iowa Caucus," Ives said.

"I'll get my bag," Marybeth said.